THE 95TH COLORED ENGINEER REGIMENT

The African-Americans who built the road to Alaska during WW II

MIKE DRYDEN

Illustrator Credit: Amanda Warren

authorHOUSE®

AuthorHouse™
1663 Liberty Drive
Bloomington, IN 47403
www.authorhouse.com
Phone: 1 (800) 839-8640

Published by AuthorHouse 12/05/2016

ISBN: 978-1-5246-2793-5 (sc)
ISBN: 978-1-5246-2791-1 (e)

Library of Congress Control Number: 2016914662

Print information available on the last page.

Any people depicted in stock imagery provided by Thinkstock are models, and such images are being used for illustrative purposes only. Certain stock imagery © Thinkstock.

This book is printed on acid-free paper.

CONTENTS

INTRODUCTION

The Jim Crow South in the 1940s was no picnic for African-Americans, and Scooter Park's life was typical. He had attended "separate but equal" public schools, grew up on land his ancestors had toiled on as slaves and worked for the "man" milking cows and picking cotton for $2.00 a day.

Scooter had grown up in North Mississippi and had managed to graduate from a segregated High School just before the Japs attacked Pearl Harbor. The early Sunday morning air raid was an unprovoked attack from a nation supposedly at peace with the US. The nation had been for non-intervention into what the news media had portrayed as a European war. Although he had been a 2nd class citizen in rural Mississippi; Scooter was proud to serve in the Army. He mustered in January of 1942 at Camp Shelby, Mississippi, about 150 miles from New Orleans, Louisiana. At the time this as far away from home he had ever been. He wrote back to his mother, Miss Mae Park that they had pine trees bigger and taller than anything he had ever seen before. But sadly, he wrote,

"Everybody in my company except for the Commanding Officer and the First Sargeant is Negro. The first night we got out

of the camp on a pass, our Sargeant had to drive us Colored boys to a small farm gas station that would serve Negros as long as they set in the back room and used the Colored only restroom."

Scooter completed his basic training and was immediately sent to train on heavy equipment like bulldozers and road graders used for road building. After a few weeks, the whole company received orders to move out.

As they were drawing TA-50 (load bearing equipment; helmets, cold weather gear, cots, sleeping bags and other field equipment), the supply clerk issued Scooter a pair of boots the likes of which he had never seen. The platoon sergeant called them mukluks and they were for cold, snowy weather climates. Little did Scooter know that very soon he would be euphoric to have these boots that Eskimos had invented.

Scooter (locals called him Scooter instead of his given name Aaron) moved out with his unit a few days later still not sure where they were heading. Anyone that's ever been in the service knows about rumors and the rumor mill was in high gear now. They were put on a train in Jackson, Mississippi in what Scooter thought was their very own special car because the Colored troops had all to themselves. A Colored conductor would bring them meals three times a day. After a day on the train, one of the guys finally asked the old Colored man where the train was heading. "Chi-Town, my man, Chi-Town," said the conductor. Somebody on the train finally told Scooter Chi-Town was Chicago, Illinois, a long way from Mississippi in more ways than one. This train trip would start Scooter on a journey that would change his life forever.

Chicago in winter 1942

The first thing Scooter noticed about the city of Chicago was none of the restaurants had any signs saying no Negros allowed, or Colored served only in the back. Scooter walked past many bars and cafes until he found one that had both Negros and white folks sitting in the same room. He gingerly and silently opened the door and walked in. As he looked around, he noticed a counter where a young, attractive Colored young lady was waiting on customers. Sheepishly, Scooter sat into an open spot and waited.

Much to Scooter's joy, the waitress walked over to him and said," What you want to eat, soldier?"

Scooter thought he had died and gone to Heaven because in the whole damn state of Mississippi, no girl he had ever seen looked as pretty as this girl. Scooter mustered up all the courage he had and said,

"Honey child, what's yo name?"

Rose replied. "You are not from around here are you, soldier boy?"

CHAPTER 1

CHICAGO IN THE WINTER OF 1942

Scooter had been taking his evening meal down at the diner where Rose worked. He used to call the evening meal supper and called the midday meal dinner. But up here they say lunch at noon and dinner at night. Scooter was working hard to shed the Mississippi slave "n....r" skin he inherited so he could become a respectable Colored man in the Windy City. He had been watching and listening how everybody acted and spoke. Colored folks had respect up here in Chi-Town. None of that ***"yes Sir Mister John and thanks you Sir for that fried chicken back"*** jive-ass talk Colored folks had to use to get by in Mississippi.

Scooter sudddenly realized," ***Hell, I ain't even seen a fried chicken back or a gizzard up here. Down home for breakfast, you would be lucky to have biscuits and red eye gravy with grits. A piece of fried fatback was only for special occasions. Damn them grits. I ain't never eating no more grits ever again. I am going come back up here after the war and go to work hard so I can serve my family white folk's food like the boss man, and the house "n....rs" eat down home."***

1

Scooter was taking a crash course in Colored Yankee city life.

He had worked up the courage to ask Rose out after a couple of weeks. He knew the unit was preparing to move out soon, and he had to court Rose proper like. Scooter had almost waited too long. Rose was being to wonder if he was interested at all. On their first date, Scooter was about as nervous as he could ever recall. He started two or three times to hold Rose's hand but chickened out at the very last minute. Rose had seen his attempts and was flattered Scooter was such a gentleman. City Colored men would take you out to a juke joint and fill you up with cheap gin. Then they would be all over you touching your private parts through your dress and trying to make out with you on your first date. If you attempted to resist, he would make a big scene talking about you being a tease and all. Yes, Rose Porter had found the man who would be her children's father. He was a little rough around the edges but inside he was gold plated.

Although he had an unfortunate beginning, his Mamma had raised him with good manners, a good work ethic and faith in God. Yes, Sir, she was going to hang on to this man.

The draft board had done let this Colored country boy off of the plantation, and he was not going back. He now called himself Aaron after Rose had told him Aaron was a name that commanded more respect than Scooter. He didn't care how many Japs or Nazis he had to kill, war couldn't be any worse than life for a Colored man in the 1940s Mississippi.

Aaron had been trying to figure out where the hell their unit was going. About every hour somebody had come up with a new location. Would they go the Pacific or go to Europe. There had been fighting in Africa, so maybe that's where we will go, not that Aaron knew where any of the places was. Being raised in Mississippi, one thing he was damn good at was doing what he was told. In the Army, they call it following orders. ***I'll be damn; Aaron thought, I been getting ready for this war all my life.***

The unit had been spending a great deal of time down at the railroad yard, loading big equipment like bulldozers and road graders. It was more to this mission than Aaron had ever known. The NCOIC (non-commissioned officer in charge) of loading quickly recognized that you only had to show Aaron Park how to do something once. After that, he not only would do his job flawlessly but would jump in without being asked to show the others how to do something. The officers and senior NCOs in Aaron's unit were all white since Army doctrine at that time reasoned that Southern Negros did not have the mental capacity to supervise anyone or the ability to work in cold climates. But there existed a language and cultural gap that only a trooper like Aaron could span. Without realizing it, Aaron had become his outfit's official liaison between the white NCOs and officers and the Colored Southern troops. They now only had to deal with Sgt. Park and they were sanguine that the job would get done right. Aaron was already an acting jack (temporary E-5) or Buck Sergeant. He didn't get any extra money, but he was proud of his new position and responsibilities. All the other men in the unit rallied behind Sgt. Park. He had a natural ability to lead. Some people said it an acquired skill, but some just have "IT." Sgt. Park had that presence about him which military leaders called "IT."

Aaron and Rose had been regularly dating and spent a great deal of time talking about family and values. Aaron shared his deepest secrets with Rose. He told Rose that he knew he lacked some of the education and social skills she and her family had. But Aaron promised if she would give him the time he would make her proud. If Rose Porter wasn't already in love with this country boy then, she was madly in love now. It was no way on earth she was going to let this young man go.

Aaron and Carrie, his baby sister, had been brought up attending the AME (African Methodist Episcopal) Church in Wren. Three times a week, once on Wednesday night for prayer meeting and twice on Sunday for morning and evening sermons, the Park family would settle down in the third pew on the right. This location was the pew where three generations of Park had sat for worship. Now, you had to want some religion to endure the hot steamy midday heat inside the AME Church in Wren, Mississippi. The Colored Funeral Home in Aberdeen (all communities big enough to have a Post Office had a Colored funeral home) always kept them supplied with big cardboard fans stapled on a flat stick. The flat stick made it possible to hold on to it even after your hands were wet with sweat. On the front would be the parlor owner's picture in color, a must for Colored Funeral Parlor Directors I reckon. On the back would be some words that were there to console you and the remaining family members in your time of grief on the passing of a loved one. Aaron, Carrie, and their Momma would always be in church, but their father had a more spotted attendance record. Even the times he did attend, the deacons would call a meeting, and the men would retire to the big oak tree outside in the gravel parking lot to drink rotgut whiskey.

Money was always tight in the Park household, but Aaron and his sister never went without any of the necessities of life. They always raised a hog or two for the fall killing and a summer vegetable garden that yielded so much produce they couldn't eat or can it all. Their Momma made a deal with the little store up the road. When the garden started coming in, she would supply the store with tomatoes, butter beans, black-eyed peas, and okra till fall when all the kids would get new shoes and clothes. It was a lot of work for $50.00 worth of shoes and clothes. If that what it took so that her kids could start school in the fall with new shoes and shirts that fit, so be it. Walking around in the summer with the toes and sides cut out of your leather shoes because your foot had outgrown them was fine. But no Park kid was going to go to school without new clothes and new shoes. The annual ritual may have been a small monetary goal, but it meant everything to their Momma. Everybody who lived in the small colored community knew all they had to do was just ask, and the Park would fill up your basket with homemade bread and fresh garden vegetables. They even picked and washed vegetables for the white folks that treated them half way right. You see, no white folks was going to be seen in a Colored folk's garden picking tomatoes and peas. Hell, that just wasn't done, don't you know.

The only exception was one white family that lived in a tenant shack right next to them. They always helped out and shared anything they had with Aaron's family. Most of the white folk just called them "White Trash" because of their situation. Poor, ill-educated, with few job skills and most important of all, no pedigree, they were just barely above the Colored folk in the Mississippi racial caste system.

Finally, after many cold weeks in Chicago, Aaron's unit got the orders to move out. The destination and mission were still a secret at least to the troops as he boarded a train for parts unknown.

Aaron broke the news to Rose and her family on last Saturday he was to be in town. The next day Aaron joined Rose and her family as he had done every Sunday for services at the Shiloh Chapel of Jesus Christ our Lord. Rose's family had regularly attended this church for over 60 years. The preacher dedicated a prayer for Aaron and all the troops headed into battle for a safe and quick return. The Reverend Holloway said when evil in this world was recognized, it was up to the God-fearing citizens of the USA to fight and destroy it.

Aaron felt a little prouder after that sermon realizing God had a larger mission on earth for him than picking cotton and hauling hay in Mississippi. The remainder of the evening was quiet and sober, given the unknown status of their soon to be son-in- law.

CHAPTER 2

THE JOURNEY TO ALASKA

The unit was standing in a company formation at the train station at 0500 hours. Sgt. Park was beginning to use the military terms for the time of day as well using some fancy foreign name for the bathroom, the latrine. Hell, the Army can call it anything they want to because it was inside the house and warm. The mess hall had been open 24 hours a day for weeks, so they got a good breakfast of fried eggs, bacon, fried apples, toast and something they called SOS. This concoction was a gravy and beef mixture you put on your toast. Man alive, Aaron thought to himself, they sure to do know how to eat up North. After getting their two boxed meals, they were off to somewhere unknown.

As the sun came up, Aaron could tell the train was headed west because the sun was at his back. The Army had taught him that at Camp Shelby, Mississippi, a place and time that now seemed so far in the past. Most of the troops were playing cards and drinking whiskey they had smuggled on the train. Drinking on duty was against regulations, but Aaron had told his troops he wouldn't be checking. He figured they had worked so hard the past month or so they deserved a little R & R. That's what the Army called rest and relaxation, a break from duty. The men deserved it. They had been thrown together months ago at Camp Shelby from all over the rural South. By now, most had just traveled as far away from their birthplace as any of their family, past and present, had since being chained and put on slave ships in West Africa 300+ years ago. Now they were all friends and would shortly have to rely on their close bond to complete their assigned mission.

Aaron settled into the quiet comfort of the warm day as he listened to the clank of the steel wheel of the train car as it moved them closer and closer to their journey's end. He used this time to write Rose. They had promised to write every day knowing Aaron's location would never be same. Aaron didn't care. He knew Rose's letters would eventfully catch up to him. The CO (commanding officer) had given Aaron an address they could use that would assure the mail would get forwarded. Aaron had written the address down on 38 separate pieces of paper to give to each of his men. He knew many of them couldn't write very well, but it was important they had something to send their kinfolks so they could keep in touch. No white NCO or Officer had told him to do it, but Aaron knew it was important.

After what seemed like a month, the train finally stopped, and they were told to disembark. Sgt. Park formed his men up, dress right dress, all standing at attention with duffle bags loaded with TA-50 beside them. Aaron had transformed into Sgt. Park a day earlier telling the men no more drinking would be allowed. He had told them, "Nobody in this here Army expects much of our unit. The last thing we need to do is to prove them white folks right. We are going to be the sharpest, hardest-working and most motivated troops in this United Stated Army. Let's be sharp, be on time and no breaking the regs. I don't know yet where we are going, but wherever we are assigned, I want us to be the best we can be. Doing our best isn't just for our pride and us. Colored folks all across the South need us to shine. We didn't have any opportunities to shine down home because the white folks thought we were dumb. Look at what we have accomplished since basic training started. How many new skills, words, and manners have we learned? Every one of us should be proud, and it ain't putting on airs to show it."

The unit broke into applause and cheers. Never before had anyone encouraged them to shoot for the moon.

As they formed up outside in front of the Pullman coaches at the train station, Sgt. Park' unit was the only one in the correct formation, clean shaven and in pressed uniforms. The CO, Cpt. Taylor looked up and down the large company formation and announced to the entire unit, "If you turn your eyes to your right you will see at the end of the formation is 1ˢᵗ platoon. They are standing at attention, uniforms on correctly and standing tall. If you Colored men want to earn respect, you need to act like you deserve it. Be like 1ˢᵗ Platoon, and you will earn that respect."

Platoon Leaders, take charge of your troops and dismiss them. That is all."

As Aaron prepared his men to move out, he saw the sign on the train depot. It said, Seattle. Aaron had heard the name but had no idea where in America it was. All he knew it was cold and wet. He could see the other men climbing into big old trucks like folks used to haul cattle and pigs to market. At least, he thought, they were covered. As they approached the trucks, they noticed a big bus just like the Trailways bus folks had up in Tupelo. Just as Sgt. Park started to marshal his men for loading, the Battalion Commander, LTC Noble, walked over to the unit with their CO, Cpt. Taylor.

"Sgt. Park."

"Yes Sir, Col. Noble."

Aaron was as scared as he had ever been because this was the first time anyone above the rank of Captain had spoken to him.

LTC Noble stretched out his hand to Sgt. Park and said,

"Son, I have had my eye on your unit since you arrived in Chicago. Your CO speaks very highly of you and the job this unit has done so far. I believe you boys need a little reward. Sgt. Park, march your men over to the bus and climb on board. Your unit is going to ride with the Officers."

Sgt. Park couldn't believe his ears, but he wasted no time in moving his men over to the bus. As they were boarding, Aaron looked briefly over at the trucks, Deuce and a halves; they called them. It seemed the trucks had positioned themselves so the troops in the back would be facing the bus. As Aaron's men were loading on the bus, he could see the disbelief in the rest of the battalion's eyes or maybe it was their jaws that had dropped to their chins. It seemed the Ole Man had "IT".

As a good leader always does, Sgt Park was the last to load. Most of the Officers were already on the bus and had given the men the thumbs up as if to signal a job well done. The Officers were seating up front, so the unit started filling up the bus from the back.

Being from the South, they were accustomed to sitting behind the white line. No Colored person would ever sit down in front of the line or a white person. It also was the custom for a Colored person to get up and move if a white person didn't have a seat. Well, as far as Aaron and his men were concerned the back was great, and a just reward for a job well done. Baby steps for now Aaron thought one thing at the time. Today ain't the time to tackle bus rides and Colored restrooms. Cpt. Taylor came on board and, even though, many open seats existed, he sat down next to Sgt. Park.

Aaron couldn't have been prouder if President Roosevelt had taken the seat.

The trip would take a couple of hours. Aaron hadn't said a word for 10 minutes. Should I say something? Aaron wondered. I don't want to step out of line after this trophy ride.

Cpt. Taylor knew he had to break the ice. He turned to his Sergeant and said.

"Sgt. Park, you ever been to Seattle before?"

"No Sir, Cpt. Taylor."

"Well, Sarge, we are headed to the Port of Tacoma. We won't be staying overnight here. A ship is waiting to transport us to Valdez, Alaska. From there we will go to Fairbanks, Alaska by convoy. I can't tell much more until the ship sails. Regulation, don't you know.

But what I can tell you is that our mission doesn't involve combat but it as important as any battle that will be fought in this war. This mission will not take over a year, but the results will outlast most things America will do in this entire war. You can tell your

men they will be able to tell their children and grandchildren that
Pappy did something helped win the war. I must be frank with you
and your men; the war is not going well for the Allies'. The Japs, of
course, have bombed Pearl Harbor; we have lost or going to lose most
every outpost in the Pacific area. The British have lost their outposts
in Hong Kong and Singapore. The Germans are bombing the hell out
of England. Most of the enemy's success is due to our side myopically
planning for peace at a time at a time when the Germans and the
Japs planning for World War ll. Bad guys never sleep, Sgt. Park. They
are planning to take over as much territory in the world as possible.
I am not telling you this to discourage you, but to inform you of the
situation our country has gotten itself into. This mission we have
been assigned will go a long way to defeating the enemy. As soon as
I can arrange a meeting after we board the ship, I will brief you, and
the other platoon sergeants and then the Ole Man will address the
entire Battalion a little later."

Aaron's head was spinning. He had just heard more
information about the war than he knew up till then. Rose's Dad had
talked to him about things in the Sunday paper, being very careful
not to talk down but to inform him a little at a time. Rose's Dad had
been educated at Jim Howard College, a prestigious post-secondary
Negro institution of higher learning. Even though Aaron didn't have
any formal education; he was smart enough to know Mr. Porter was
giving him an education without making him feel stupid. This kind
gesture had endeared Rose's ole man to Aaron. Mr. Porter was paying
him more attention than his worthless whiskey-soaked own Dad had
ever done. The only attention Aaron's ole man ever paid to him was
when he gave a whipping with his belt. All of those things Mr. Porter
had said now made sense. The pressure Aaron felt was greater than
any time is his entire life. No, the Ole Man hadn't discouraged him
but put a passion in his soul that would remain there a lifetime. This

war is bigger than just us. He had to make damn sure his family and friends in Mississippi and Rose's family in Chicago never see a Jap or German attacking the homeland.

Aaron thought*, No, sir. That's not going to happen on my watch.*

As the unit arrived at the Port of Tacoma, Aaron could see the bulldozers, trucks, and road graders being loaded on the ship. He couldn't even remember ever seeing a picture of a ship this big.

The bus with all the officers and Aaron platoon arrived first. Cpt. Taylor told Aaron to form up his men and march over to ramp that leads to the ship.

Cpt. Taylor said,

"You guys get onboard and pick your billeting area. It will be about 30 minutes before the rest of the Battalion is ready to board. That few extra minutes should give you all enough time to get settled and find the chow hall. Don't worry about the time. When everybody gets settled and fed, I'll brief you and the other platoon leaders on the mission."

Sgt. Park saluted the CO and proceeded to do as ordered. As the men climbed the stairs, each and everyone was in awe of the size of the ship and the port. The trip was virgin ground for these country Colored men from the South. *Just wait till I write home and tell them about this. Yes sir, draw a line on the ledger coz this is going to be a new and exciting adventure.*

A steward directed the men to their quarters. As they approached the troop billets, he turned and said to the men,

"You guys sure are lucky to get on board the ship first because there is only one room large enough for your whole unit. It has its separate head and shower. You get real beds, not the hammocks most of the rest of them will have to sleep on. Most of the others will wander around the lower deck for the first few days trying to learn their way around. You guys are lucky since all you got to do from this room is turn right and follow the aroma to the chow hall. One thing this ship has going for it is great chow. You can eat all you want, and it's open all day and night. There's always ice cream, cake, and pie available with lots of tea, milk, coffee and soda to wash it down. If there's anything else you need, just you holler. The Captain of this ship will do anything for you troops. He was Captain of a Navy ship in the last war, and he wants to do his part to make your trip a pleasure. Your towels and supplies are in the head. Just put your towels in the container and fresh ones will be provided the same day. See you all later."

Everybody settled in, found a bunk and told Sgt. Park they were ready for the chow hall. Aaron led the way, and as he turned into the chow hall, he couldn't believe his eyes. He had never seen such a spread. As they moved down the line, the cooks offered them ham, fried chicken, roast beef, turkey and stuffing with gravy. If you wanted more than one, you just had to ask. By this time, all of them gotten to the end of the serving line and most everybody's plate was overflowing. As if they didn't have enough to eat, the dessert counter came into view. Now Aaron had been at many a sermon and dinner on the ground at the AME Church of Wren, but this was in a class of its own.

Everyone sat down and immediately began to chow down. Not a word was uttered except for a few remarks about how good all these fixings were. When the men slowed down, Aaron began to speak,

"Men, the Captain told me a lot about this war and how we are doing, and it's not good news. I don't remember all the places he mentioned, but you all know about the Japs attacking Pearl Harbor. But a lot more is going on. Over in Europe, the Nazis are bombing England, and the Japs done run over some other places where we have military bases. We are just getting started fighting. The Captain told me where we are going but not why. He said the battalion commander would brief us after we set sail. I believe we will sail in a few hours. We are going to Alaska. We are going to stop at some port and drive the equipment by convoy. I did remember where it was going. It's a town called Fairbanks. We all will find out about our mission, but the Captain said it's not fighting but is real important. He said all our kids and grandkids would be able to say their grandpappies did something important that help win the war. I don't about the rest of you, but no Nazi or no Jap is going to hurt my family."

"Amen Sarge, Amen," they all said.

CHAPTER 3

THE MISSION IN ALASKA

The Captain had called for a platoon leader's meeting in the mission briefing room. Sgt. Park has just settled into a big leather chair finer than anything he had ever seen when Cpt. Taylor walked into the room. Sgt. Park jumped up and stood at attention and yelled, "Attention!" All the men jumped up as if something had stung them in the butt. Cpt. Taylor had a little smile on his face. He knew he had made the correct decision when he promoted Aaron to Sergeant. He turned to his staff and said,

"Men, we are now under way, and I can reveal to you our mission. First, let me set the stage by giving you an update on the war situation. As we all know the Japs, Nazis and Italians are our enemies. Our side is called the Allies. Our allies are the British Commonwealth, which includes England, Scotland, Australia and Canada. Russia and some disposed leaders of occupied nations like France and the Netherlands are on our side. Our automobile plants are now weapon factories and are operating 24 hours a day basis to turn all the war materials needed to sustain what looks to be a long, bloody war. Russia is in need of aircraft, and our pilots need to ferry them to Fairbanks, Alaska. Our unit will build a road from Dawson Creek, British Columba, Canada to Delta Junction, Alaska, which is 100 miles east of Fairbanks through some uncharted and rugged territory. Survey teams have been deployed already to begin marking the road. It will be built similarly to the Transcontinental Railroad with crews starting at both ends and meeting in the middle. Our section will commence in Fairbanks Alaska. Once this road is open, troops and supplies can be transported to our bases in Alaska. Also, those aircraft will have refueling points all along this Alaska-Canada Highway. The Chiefs of Staff at the War Department in Washington believe a grave threat exists for a land invasion by Japan in Alaska. This road will link Alaska to the contiguous United States for the first time since we purchased the territory from the Russians. As you can see, our mission is very crucial to the war effort. This type of effort is called a strategic mission. I know some of you wanted to go into combat. Trust me when I tell you, all of you will eventually get to a combat zone. I have been told that the bugs and mosquitoes are as large as crows in Alaska. The weather will be cold and wet most of the time even in the summer. We will begin construction in early in the Alaskan spring. The ground has what the engineers call permafrost that means some of the ground never thaws. What makes this condition important for us is, as the sun warms and thaws the top of the soil, the surface just below is hard as a rock. As soon as you run road equipment over this surface, you have mud. The more of the surface melts, the deeper the mud gets, making moving big equipment slower. To make matters worse, the frozen earth we will have to move will need to cut up with the bulldozers. We will have to adapt to this untested road construction method. No one is saying this project will easy but as the Ole Man will tell the rest of the troops tonight, succeed we must. The safety of the nation and all of our families are at stake. I have trained and observed you and your men for many months. Army doctrine before the war dictated Colored troops could only be assigned warm regions because the brass felt Colored people from the South couldn't adapt. It's a lot of things that fall in the "Colored people can't do it" category, but you and your troops can start to change that view one piece at a time. Remember when times get hard, and you are sore, cold and tired, press on because Colored folks all over the South are counting on you.

If there are no questions, then you are dismissed until the Ole Man's briefing."

Aaron felt like for the first time in his life; he would be able to show white folks he was as good as them. He was determined to instill in his men the same passion. As he walked into the platoon room, everybody was spread out on their bunks talking, writing letters home or losing their pay by gambling with the fancy city "n....r"s from New Orleans. You could hear small talk and the noise created by the creaking of the bedsprings of the bunks. But as soon as Aaron opened the door, the room fell silent. One of the men said.

"Sarge, where we are going and what is we gonna be doing?"

Aaron became Platoon Sergeant Park, pulled out his notebook and said to his men,

"Boys, I was only able to tell you a little about our mission at chow, but now I got the whole story. The Brass in Washington says we need a road to Alaska so some planes can be refueled on their way to Alaska before being flown on to Russia. You see them planes require gas and without a road, no trucks can get the gas to the planes. Also, the Captain said they feared an Alaskan invasion from the Japs. Did you know you can't drive from here in these United States to Alaska? Well, that's where we come in. You know how I am with some names but from that town they call Fairbanks, us and about 10,000 others are going to build a 1500 mile road to Canada. After we finish this highway, they can take gas and food to the boys in Alaska. Now I forgot what word the Captain used to describe our mission. But what it meant was it would help the war in the long run and for years to come it would be something we could be proud. It will be something to brag about when we get home and some day to our kids and grandkids. Imagine when we get back to our families and the man in the big house come up and says, "Well, boy what did you do in the War?" You can tell him that you built a road to Alaska. You could tell him looks likes he just got fatter and dumber, but I don't think it would be a good idea. Something else the Captain said you all should know. It seems the higher ups don't believe we have a lot of brains and us from the South can't work in the cold. Now, I know you feel like I do about that crap. If Colored folks have put up with sorry ass white folks crap for over 300 years, we can put with any amount of grief they can throw at us. Now you know how it is, white folks get the ham, and we get the chitlins. The white folks gets the fried chicken breasts, and we get the backs and gizzards, I don't expect it's going to be any different up here. White folks gets a house, and we gets a tent. They gets hot food, and we gets sardines. You know everybody is going to be looking at us. You may not know it now, but this war could be our chance to shows them white folks what we can do. We got to work harder, longer, with crappier equipment and live in worst conditions than the white troops. If you need to bitch, bitch at me. Remember, they don't expect us to be able to do anything. Hell, we ought to thank those Japs. It got our black asses out of Mississippi, and I am not going back.

The voyage was smooth and steady. The large blue water vessel cut through the Alaska Inside Passage like a hot knife through butter. The noise from the large diesel engines was noisy at first, but now it was like your Mama singing a lullaby to you. Man, you can sleep like a baby. Every day the steward brought in clean sheets and towels while they were below deck checking the equipment's tie downs and dunnage. Aaron noticed the other platoons were washing down the decks, painting or some other kind of "make-do" work projects. Captain Taylor had persuaded the Ole Man to let him give Aaron's platoon light duty in the morning and free personal time in the afternoon. He was sure grateful to that white Officer. No white man had ever treated him as good in Mississippi. Come to think of it, several of the white man's wives had been kind to him and other Colored folks so long as the Big Bossman wasn't around. Aaron remembered several times when Miss Lottie Mae Malone, who was Mister John Malone Misses, treated him almost like a white man until that beer drinking pot bellied bastard would come into the room. She would give us a look like she was saying she was sorry and would then say something like,

"Now get on back to work, boy. Mister John ain't paying you to drink cool well water in the shade."

You could see Mister John smile with pride, knowing he had taught her everything she knew about keeping the Colored help in line. Aaron realized that Mr. John's wife could show him a thing or two if given the chance.

Being first in line at the chow hall was a real treat to these Colored men from the South. Being first in the chow line was the only time since they were a kid that they got the first pass at the food. Most of the time, it was "*let your little sister eat first*" or "*let Missy Betsy have that pork chop"*. The one he hated the most was, *"Let Preacher Moses have all he wants to eat before you even come to the table."*

Take an ole cold tater and wait, my ass. Those days are over for me. From now on, I am going to eat, talk and act like Rose's family in Chicago. Aaron was going to stand tall and be proud of his Color.

Aaron especially liked to walk on the deck and look at the mountains and islands as the ship make its way to port. Somewhere about the 5th or 6th day, Aaron was just marveling at how damn pretty this land was when something rolled out of the water like a big ole Tombigbee River mud cat. But it weren't no catfish, too damn big and was blowing water or steam out of his back. This big ass fish was so big he couldn't even get all the way out of the water like a bass or a perch when it rolled on its side and splashed back into the water. Aaron looked around, to see if anybody else had seen it, but nobody was on deck. Damn, no one is going to believe this fish tale. His heart beat was still racing when up ahead in this big inlet was the largest piece of ice he had ever seen. Sure, back home in Wren they had a couple of days a year between hog killing and spring planting, it got chilly. Puddles of muddy water would freeze up at night but by dinnertime, it would be a mud hole again. But this ice was higher than those tall buildings in Chicago where Rose's Dad worked. Now Mr. Porter had told him about even bigger and taller one's downtown, but he hadn't seen them personally. Man, the ice went all the way around the sides of the inlet and so far up in the mountains he couldn't see the end of it. The water was the prettiest blue you would ever hope to see, and fish were jumping everywhere.

There were big birds just soaring in the sky above the water. Aaron thought it must be one of those eagles he had heard about in the 11th grade. But Miss Davis never told the class how big, and majestic these eagles were. Just as Aaron had got lost in his thoughts, that eagle swooped down hitting the water going 90 miles an hour or so. Just when Aaron was sure that dumb ass bird had done gone and killed himself, out of the water, that eagle came with a fish in its mouth, flew over to this island and landed in a tree. It must have a nest because it was a big bundle of sticks and such. Just about the time the ship was slipping past the ice, a hulk of it fell off the size of a hay barn, hell maybe two hay barns. That ice threw water up in the air higher than that fish. Now the temperature on deck according to the chart on the chow hall bulletin board was 45 degrees. But that wind in your face made it feel colder than he had ever been. Man, Aaron thought to himself,

"This ain't no weather for a Colored man from Mississippi."

Aaron was determined to find out what kind of fish that was so he wandered around until he found a deck hand he had met earlier. Jim was from Chicago and was much older than Aaron. Aaron knew he could be trusted not to make fun of him, so he asked him about the big fish. Jim told him it weren't no fish but a whale. *Not a fish my ass, I saw the damn thing, it was swimming in the water like a fish, went under water like a fish so don't tell me it ain't no damn fish.* But Aaron had learned to shut his mouth and listen cause his Mamma had said you can't learn anything if you are running your mouth. She uses to say, "Boy, the Good Lord gave you two ears and one mouth so he must have meant for you to listen twice as much as you talk." So he listened as Jim explained that a whale was something they call a mammal, like you, a dog or a moose. Jim said this time of year they leave Hawaii and swim up here to breed. He also asked Jim about that big piece of ice. Jim told him they were called glaciers and had been around for thousands of years. Jim proudly told Jim that he saw a big hulk fall off while he was watching so in a couple of days it ought to be all gone. Jim just looked at Aaron and said, "Maybe you're right, young man, maybe you're right."

As Aaron made his way back to the squad room, he reflected all he had seen since leaving that poor ass dirt farm and a wood shack in North Mississippi. Here he was in charge of a platoon of soldiers, on a ship to Alaska and was fixing to build a road so you can drive from the United States to Alaska. He decided to share what he just saw with his men, after all. As he walked into the room, he announced,

"Get your coats on and follow me. I know none of you sorry ass Colored boys has ever seen a whale or a glacier, let alone an eagle. Your platoon sergeant is going to educate you."

The men followed Sgt. Park up on deck where he explained that these big fish called whales done swum from Pearl Harbor up here just to breed. Folks say these formations of ice called glaciers are thousands of years old. Now not long after they arrived on deck, a whale breached the water's surface and came thundering down just 50 yards from where they were standing. Aaron had never seen these Colored boys unable to speak apart from for the bus trip to the ship with the White Officers.

After what seemed like a month (just 12 days), the ship docked in Valdez, Alaska after turning into something the ship Captain called Prince William Sound. Aaron wondered why a prince would live in this cold ass place, but he guessed if you were a prince, you could act a fool, and nobody would say a word. Some little flat looking boats called tugs met them and ran alongside the ship. Then they helped the ship's skipper get up close to the dock. Aaron didn't have to tell his men to pack up because they had been ready to put their Colored feet on solid ground. When they marched down the gangway, they could see nothing but snow. Sure he had seen snow in Wren, Mississippi, once in '36 and again in '39. But damn, the snow here was piled up as high as the second floor of the houses. Little puffs of white smoke curled out of stovepipes on the roofs and dogs were barking as they assembled in company formation in the clear area by the gangway. Aaron thought to himself, *crazy ass white folks think they can build a road in the snow. No wonder they brought us ole Colored boys from the South up here to work. They a betting we don't know any better, but we do.*

Captain Taylor had been briefed not to keep the men in company formation too long because of the extreme cold. He told his Platoon Leaders to have the men stow their gear in the deuce and a half trucks and march them to their quarters. The temperature was 20 degrees, but the wind was a blowing hard off the water with little hard bits of ice in it. One of the deck hands said it had been a mild winter, only 14 feet of snow. Mild my ass Aaron thought, *I hate to be in a bad winter. By now in Mississippi, we would have tomatoes vines 6 inches tall along with some butter beans and red radishes.*

The unit settled into the big metal barn where they kept airplanes. No soft mattresses and a steward to bring you towels in this place. Chow had taken a hit too. They gave everyone three days of K-rations and a P-38 (that was what the Army called a can opener). Since it was getting dark and cold, the Captain had told Aaron to bed down the men for the night. One of the other platoons had been assigned night guard duty, so they caught a break. It had been a long day, so most of the men settled in and called it a night.

Aaron was up the next morning before the rest of the platoon so he could find the Captain for his road march orders. As he was walking toward the ship, he saw Captain Taylor and LTC Noble standing on the docks watching the equipment being offloaded. Aaron made sure he was where the Captain could see him because you just didn't walk up to an Officer without being summoned. Fortunately, the Captain saw Sgt. Park and motioned for him to come over. Aaron walked over to the two Officers, snapped to attention, rendered a salute and said,

"Good morning Sirs. Sure is a fine day."

"Good morning to you Sergeant Park. Did you and your men get rations for the next few days?' said Captain Taylor.

"Yes Sir, the men will be packed up and ready to go in an hour," Aaron told his CO.

Aaron had been directed to the staging area where all the equipment had been marshaled overnight. Aaron thought,

These folks must want this road built fast because they ain't letting the sun set on any of our black asses in any port.

As the convoy pulled out of Valdez headed north to Fairbanks, one thing was clear to Aaron. Alaska was colder and snowier than he had ever been taught in school. The trucks pulling the road equipment looked to be as wide as the road. Aaron was being generous even calling this little strip of clearing a road. Hell, back home the cows made a better trail to the milk barn than this little path in the woods. All the snow on the side of the road was higher than the tops of the trucks. Won't just know it, just as the convoy pulled out it a started to snow so hard the damn wipers on the truck couldn't keep the windshield clean. It didn't matter because it was snowing too hard to see much down the road anyhow. Every time you let your foot off the gas pedal or push it down, the damn wipers would stop moving. To top it off the top of the cab was covered in a green tarp like you would cover up hay in the field. There was no heater that we could find, maybe it's one of those switches on the dash, but me and the driver ain't got any time to play around. What fool thought this up? I bet his ass is warm and inside an office with hot coffee while we are trying to make our way up this pig trail in the blinding snow. Aaron's unit was the lead platoon, so he had a radio to talk to the CO. He called to inform him about the road conditions. The CO said the Ole Man had expected it to be slow going so just be safe. He said 15 minutes from now the convoy would start the climb a hill. The CO told him they would drive up and over this place called Thompson Pass so be very careful not to stop for any reason.

Aaron thought we got hills in Mississippi so what so damn important about this one. Hell. Cotton Gin Hill is the biggest hill he had ever seen in North Mississippi so that this hill couldn't be any higher. It wasn't possible.

Well, Aaron was wrong. He could feel the truck start to labor as they drove up the hill. He looked up the road to try to see the top, but the clouds went all the way down to the ground so he couldn't see the crest. They drove for almost an hour when a big ravine came up on his left, and he couldn't see the top of the hills up that draw. But what he did see was a butt load of snow come sidling off the side of the mountain. It was kicking up snow back up into the clouds. It looked like it was going to make it to the road. So Aaron picked up the radio and called Captain Taylor, "Sir, we almost up to the top of that place. But there is this big wave of snow just barreling ass down this here hill on our left. It looks like it headed for the road!"

"Sgt Park put the gas pedal to the metal floorboard and don't you stop for anything! Do you understand! yelled the CO.

"Yes Sir, Wilco, out."

Aaron turned to tell his driver to get the hell out of here, but the Cajun Colored driver hadn't waited. Southern Colored man or not, he knew the wall of snow is coming at them wasn't good. Aaron had concerns about the rest of the convoy. All he knew was stopping wasn't a good idea, so he barreled up the road till the saw the top. He was glad to start downhill, but he thought he should call the CO.

"Sir, This Sgt Park and we have cleared the top and are headed down. Should we stop or keep going?"

Aaron waited for a reply for a minute. Maybe this radio is out of range or something he mused. He picked up the mike again and called, "Captain Taylor, this is Sergeant Park, come in, over!"

Aaron was getting frantic to speak to anyone in the convoy so he could find out what had happened to the rest of the convoy. The last order he received from his CO was to drive as fast as he could so that was what he was going to do till somebody called him. They headed down the pass and were going faster than he knew his driver could handle.

"Better slow this rig down Trooper, or you'll never eat gumbo again." Aaron cautioned his driver.

"Yes Sarge, I was getting worried about driving so fast on the ice and snow. I ain't never seen this kind of weather down on the bayou. I sure to miss grits, cathead biscuits and redeye gravy my

Mamma used to fix. The food on the ship was good, but a body has got to have home cooking ever so often."

Aaron just smiled and nodded his head as to say "I heard that."

"Sgt Park, This is Captain Taylor, over." Aaron was sure glad to hear that white man's voice.

"Sgt. Park here Sir."

"Good to hear you made it over the pass and managed to miss the avalanche. Can you tell how far you have driven since the crest of the pass?" Captain Taylor asked.

"Yes Sir, we have driven about 14 miles, Sir."

"Good job Sarge. By the way, these radios only work if you have a line of sight, so if we are on opposite side of the mountain, we won't be able to talk so don't get worried. It looks everyone in our company made it pass the slide, but I'm not sure about the rest of the convoy. The snow was getting close to the road as we passed. Our orders are to proceed to a small settlement called Gulkana. There will be road guards to guide you into parking. We'll talk later if something changes. And before I forget, that was one hell of a job getting the whole company over the mountain pass. It would have been a disaster if you had stopped. We all would have been buried under the snow. Always remember to follow your last order no matter what."

"Yes Sir, thank you, Sir."

Since everyone had been issued K-rations back at the port, Aaron's men got to eat when they wanted to. These K-rations were in green tin cans. Aaron wasn't sure after a couple of meals if the can was to keep germs out or the food inside. The Lucky Strike and the Camel cigarette folks had put a little pack of smokes in the box. Free smokes were a good deal for the men that smoked because they hadn't been paid since they left Chicago and most were flat broke. Of course, some had a bunch of money won from fools stupid enough to shoot dice with the two fancy city Negros from New Orleans. Yea those slick city Colored boys done schooled the country boys.

One treat in the K-rations box was a piece of chocolate shaped like a flat stone you would skip across a pond. It was so hard you could bust off a tooth trying to bit off a portion. But if you stuck it in your shirt pocket for a while, you could use it as a scoop in your peanut butter.

That's some kind of good. Somebody ought to make a candy bar with peanut butter and chocolate and sell it. I knows I would buy it for Rose and our kids. Man, I sure do long for Miss Rose Porter, the future Mrs. Park, and mother of a bunch of our kids. I can't wait until this damn ole war is over so we start us a family.

After about an hour, the snow began to lighten up, and they started to see some of the most beautiful countryside they had even laid their eyes. Even Miss Davis at the Wren Colored School never showed them pictures of anything like this land. Snow covered the mountains; ice covered all the rivers, creeks and ponds as well as anything else outside. Man, how do these people live up here all the time? I bet they freeze their asses off. Hell, it was already springtime everywhere else in the world. Aaron thought this would be a good time for a little sunshine to help melt all this ice. Rose is never going to believe this story so maybe the Army had somebody to take pictures. They seemed to have someone assigned for taking pictures of everything else. Just as they topped a big hill, a moose and some of his friends that were walking in the middle of the road popped into sight.

"Holy Smokes (but he didn't say Smokes)" Aaron screamed as they looked like they were going to hit all of them head-on.

But at the last second, the moose trotted off the road and gave them a steely stare, the likes of which Aaron or his driver had never seen on an animal. Now down home in Mississippi they had deer, but these moose were three or four times bigger. Or maybe it was because Aaron's eyes were wider than ever before or maybe it's all that blood his heart was a pumping. It was four or five miles further down the road (which was north) before Aaron got his breath and heartbeat slowed down enough to speak "Good job driving, Trooper. Most folks would have panicked, but you did just fine."

"What were those, big ass deer?"

"No, those were moose. According to the Cpt. Taylor, we will see a lot of them while we are here. Judging by the look on its face, maybe we should just let them walk where ever the hell they want."

After driving all day (which was considerably shorter than most places), they arrived at this settlement called Gulkana. The CO had told Aaron just to follow the road guides that wasn't hard since they had marked the road with flares, and all the MPs had flashlights. Thank God the first day was over. That's one day down and two to go until they reached Fairbanks.

These MPs had thought of everything. They lined us up so we could refuel right away, something we won't have to do in the morning in the dark and cold. The Army always started the day off in the dark. I got to sleep later back home when I helped Mr. Randy with his milk cows, but I ain't on the farm no more. After the trucks had been staged for the next day, an MP signaled at Aaron to come over. As he approached the MP said to Aaron,

"Sarge, get your men off the truck and into a unit formation. I will escort you to your quarters for the night. Bring your TA-50 because you will need it." Well, meals were not a problem cause they still had two days worth of K-Rats left over.

As the MP stopped the convoy and motioned to two large tents, Aaron thought to himself,

"First, the chow went to hell and now the quarters. Floors were covered with straw no self-respecting mule would touch and at one end was a trash can somebody had made into a stove. It was most certainly a downgrade from the ship. Well, at least we'll be warm."

How wrong Aaron was. It was 25 degrees below zero and the sun had just set.

Aaron got his men settled in and went to the CO's platoon leaders meeting. As he was walking over to the headquarter building, he noticed the convoy was still coming in from the port.

He thought to himself; *I hope no one got hurt on that hill.* He could tell the bulldozers had been offloaded to move some snow because the snow had frozen to the tracks and blades. Aaron made his way past all the tents, trucks, fuel drums and various equipment until he reached HQ. As he walked into the room, the warmth hit him in the face.

Man, this is the first time since we left the ship my ole bones are warm, Aaron mused. Naturally, this was where all the white officers were staying. Some things never change, but he was glad at least he now knew how the other half lived. Aaron was making mental notes for the post-war ex-Sergeant Park.

The CO had the men sit at a large table in his quarters. Just as they were settling in, a strange looking man entered the room with sacks of hamburgers, fries, and cold drinks. All the platoon leaders looked at the man as if he was from another planet, but the expression on his face was every bit as puzzling. He wasn't exactly white and sure enough wasn't no Colored man lessen his folks had broken all the rules they had down in Mississippi. You could get your Colored ass hung for just whistling at a white woman. God only knows what the Klan would if you knocked a white woman up.

After the man had left, the CO said,

"Chow down, dinner is on me tonight. I wanted to tell you how pleased I was with today's convoy movement. The other units weren't as lucky. Several stopped on the pass making the entire remaining convoy to stop dead in their tracks. The avalanche covered the road, buried three trucks and pushed them off the road. The cleanup crews will be coming in all night.

Tomorrow we will pull out at 0530 hours so have your men up and packed by 0500. I will depend on you platoon leaders to get this done. Our trip tomorrow will be to Delta Junction. We will stop overnight, refuel and proceed to Fairbanks the next morning. I will brief on more details tomorrow night. The trip from Delta Junction to Fairbanks is about 110 miles, and the road doesn't get any better. We can thank God it's mostly flat so we will not have to traverse another Thompson Pass. I thought it better not to brief you on the mountain pass operations since most of you grew up driving down on the farm and would react to the conditions. You did a great job. And, by the way, I noticed all of you looking at the man that brought in the hamburgers. He was an Alaskan Eskimo and believe me when I tell you; he had just seen his first Colored man. So don't be alarmed if some of his buddies come by to see you. It's only been 10 minutes but by now the whole village knows about you. Just be nice because these people have no prejudices toward Colored men so make a good impression. If no one has any questions, then you are dismissed. Have a good night."

As the troops left the HQ, Captain Taylor wondered,

"I wonder what these men would think if they knew I was a quarter Negro."

His grandparents lived in a small upstate hamlet in Vermont; the marriage union didn't raise any eyebrows. What he worried about was what would happen if any of the white Officers found out. Captain Taylor's Granny was a light Colored woman so he didn't inherit any of the dark skin. Most of these Officers were sent here under orders; many were just screw ups that in a nonwartime situation would never have seen an Officer's commission. LTC Noble wasn't like the rest, but he knew he was swimming upstream trying to integrate the Colored troops into the white engineers' battalions. You could forget about any help from the War Department since it was Army doctrine that stated no Southern Colored troops would serve in a cold weather climate. Also, nothing but a white officer would command a Colored unit. I guess the Japs changed the cold weather policy at Pearl Harbor last December. Captain Taylor decided just to keep a low profile and do what he could do. He owed his Granny that much.

Back at the Native village

Later that night, the young man who delivered the food gathered up some the men and women of the village to tell them about the "Midnight Men" camped on the tundra at the filling station. He started out by saying,

"These people with the white soldiers were like us except black like the sky at midnight. I have never seen anyone like them before. They sounded like the white ones but were different. They seemed like they didn't want to be here."

"You lie, Thomas. You are always telling tales. You will make a good elder storyteller one day, but you just make stuff up." Admonished his cousin, Nochuck.

"If you don't believe me, then I will show you."

"I'm not going across the road until the white man leaves." Bellowed Nochuck as he crossed his arms with a huff.

"Then you will be waiting a long time, my friend. Come, go with me tonight." His cousin replied.

Thomas was making no headway with his cousin. The ole ways or the highway was Nochuck's motto. But human nature is universal.

Just as Thomas was about to go back to the Army camp alone, his wife said,

"Nana and I want to see the Midnight Men. They will leave soon and never come back. Tonight will be our only chance."

Nana was Thomas's sister-in-law and wife to the stubborn one, Nochuck.

Nochuck, not to be shown up by his wife in front of his in-laws and friends said,

"I will go to protect you from the White and Midnight Men. No woman of mine will ever see another man without me."

'Nana quickly, politely but firmly told her husband,

"Nochuck, I let you get away with your big talk around other men from the village but in my house, you will respect my wishes. You, of course, may come with me. It is I who will protect you from doing something that will bring shame and dishonor to our village. Understand?"

Nochuck, having been properly put in his place, wisely agreed to his wife's terms. Even Nochuck could make a wise decision when his options were explained to him.

Nana and Thomas' wife Alissa were sisters and very much alike. Thomas, Alissa, and Nana had the explorer spirit, but Nochuck didn't. He preferred to sit in the village and talk about the poor fish run and the wildfire that destroyed the berry plants. Years earlier, the three explorers had set out to parts unknown to find berries and some new sources of fish. After a week's hike, they found glorious and ample berry bushes, freshwater fish, and more moose than they could count. They stayed so long at the new hunting grounds, some of the men came looking for them. The villagers expected to find the explorer trio dead and eaten by wolves. But instead, they found they had set up camp to process all the bounty. The search party set down to feast, the likes of which, they had never seen. A freshly harvested moose hung by the shelter. Bears had come up to eat the harvested moose and were killed, skinned and butchered. The three had built a smoking room as well as a drying rack. The doors were bear hides, the product of too nosey bears. New types of fish hung carefully on the racks and a front quarter of the moose was cooking. They all sat down to an impromptu feast after telling the three of them how happy they were to seeing them. A runner was sent back to Gulkana to tell the anxious villagers the good news. Even Nochuck, who had given them up for dead, came to see them. When he saw his wife, Nana, he embraced her **IN FRONT OF THE OTHER MEN.** He told her he was so happy to see her, and her babies missed her as well.

Nochuck never questioned his wife's judgment again.

This new place became the village's new summer camp. No longer did they have to worry about the competition from the invading soldiers who had to kill animals and catch fish to survive, too.

As Thomas, Alissa, Nana, and Nochuck approached the Army encampment, a sentry stopped them and challenged them. Thomas explained he had delivered the hamburgers to the Midnight

Men and the white officer earlier had his permission to visit the tents of the Colored soldiers. The private had no authority to grant entry into the camp without orders from some higher ups. He told them they would have to leave. The disappointment on their faces convinced him to escort them to the Captain Taylor's quarters. With the CO's blessings, the Natives were escorted to the Colored soldier's tent. After the troops had been instructed to act like their Mamma and minister were in the room, the Alaska Natives meet the Midnight Men from the South.

Sgt. Park greeted them at the door and introduced the squad to the Native Alaskans. Aaron had never seen his men's eyes as wide as they were upon seeing "***the new people.***" Well, except maybe, when they saw the whale on the trip aboard the ship on the voyage. Thomas, always the curious one, asked where they were born. They all started calling out their hometowns all at once, each trying to yell louder than the last person. This sort of behavior scared the natives because they weren't accustomed to loud talking and the rude manners the black troops displayed. Culture clash had come to both the Colored Southern soldiers and the Native Alaskans. What is acceptable behavior in one culture may be considered rude in another culture.

After the initial encounter, the conversation began.

One soldier from the Bayou country in Louisiana asked," What kind of fish do you catch up here?"

Thomas said, "We catch salmon in our fish wheels and trout in our nets. We dry and smoke them, so we have food for the winter our families and our dog teams will need."

"You feed fish to a dog! I ain't never seen no dog eat a fish, but I have seen them chase down rabbits and squirrels. Seems like a waste of fishes."

"Maybe so, but the dogs are how we travel in the winter. We have no other way except to walk." Thomas replied.

Another soldier said, "I thought us Colored boys had it bad down South! At least I can drive the farm tractor over to the general store when I wants something."

The conversation went on for hours, with each group finally realizing they weren't that different, just looked a little different. Aaron's biggest problem was to keep some of his oversexed young soldiers from insulting their guests with some inappropriate remarks about the women.

Sgt Park finally decided to call an end to the encounter since 0500 hours was just a few short hours away. The natives and the Colored said their goodbyes before parting ways. The Colored soldiers were amazed how these people could live up here in this cold dark place.

Never before in any of their past had such a culture diversity lesson occurred. Back at the village the next morning, everybody wanted to hear about the midnight men.

CHAPTER 4

THE ADVENTURE CONTINUES

The trip to Delta Junction went without any complication, and the convoy arrived on schedule. The lodging was the same green tents with straw on the frozen ground just like in Gulkana. You can always bet the Army will make one place look just like the last. Everything had to be uniform, dress right dress, spic and span don't you know. I bet you could charge a Jap machine gun nest, kill twenty Japs soldiers with a pocket knife and save a General, and all he would say was,

"Boy, where's your helmet? Don't you know you're out of uniform?"

The trucks were refueled and marshaled for the trip to Fairbanks the next morning.

The drive to Fairbanks the next day took only five hours, so they arrived at Ladd Field by about noon. All Aaron saw was more snow, a couple of airplanes and more tents. But one of those tents had a sign that read "Mess Hall."

Hot chow was the way to a soldier's heart. These men would even eat some of that SOS that they were fed on the ship. After the trucks had been marshaled, Captain Taylor called for a Platoon Leaders meeting at base operations (or Base Ops for seasoned soldiers).

"Men, this is the start of our mission. We are going to build a 1500 mile road to Dawson City, British Columbia, Canada from Delta Junction, Alaska linking Alaska to the lower 48 states road system. We are going to spend several days checking out our equipment, drawing some more cold weather gear before moving to begin the construction phase. Some engineers from Caterpillar Company will make some modifications to the bulldozers so your operators will need to be handy to offer assistance. There are two Colored engineers that I am sure will be glad to speak to you about life out of the South. As soon as you are dismissed, get your men to the chow hall. Brief your men on the subjects I've covered and remember don't let any of the white troop's goat you into a fight. I'll not tolerate any fights. Understand?"

Captain Taylor dismissed his men. As they filed out, he wondered if he should tell them what's in store. Maybe it's best not to overwhelm them at the start of this yearlong project.

Aaron sensed uneasiness about Captain Taylor's demeanor he had not seen in the past. His atypical behavior set Aaron to wonder what the CO was holding back. Well, no matter, cause Aaron doesn't always tell his men everything at once. Some get confused, and some get down in the mouth, so he gives them little bits of information while being sure not to lie.

The Mess Hall was a welcome sight. The cooks had plenty of chow, and you got all you could fit in your mess kit. The only problem was you had to go outside to eat. Somebody said the temperature was 15 degrees, but the wind made it seem colder. For the next meal, Aaron would make sure the stoves in the tents were fired up so at least they could eat in a warm place. However, that would be for the night chow. Right now, it was a race just to eat before the damn food froze to the metal mess kit. Aaron didn't realize that this situation would be the best he and his men would see until they left Alaska.

Aaron told his men to follow him over to three trash cans filled with hot water so they could clean their mess kits. Some of the platoon members followed Aaron but most didn't. In basic training, all of the men had been trained to clean the mess kits after chow, but that had been a long time ago.

Work began on the bulldozers soon after chow. Aaron's platoon was assigned one of the Colored engineers from Caterpillar Company named James Elmore.

James held a personal interest in these Colored troops. His parents were originally from Inverness, Mississippi in the Mississippi Delta, a land lost in the antebellum days of Dixie and a place even a Native white non-Delta born Mississippian needed a passport to enter. As his Dad once told him,

"I loaded up you and your mother in a $100 truck with a full tank of gas, $20, got on Highway 61 headed north and never looked back."

Fortunately for his Daddy, the truck ran out of gas in Peoria, Illinois. At a gas station, where he stopped to put in his last $4.00 in the tank for gas, a Colored gentleman came over and said,

"You're a long way from home, ain't you?"

"Yes Sir, I am."

"You don't have to Sir me. Peoria ain't Mississippi, and a Colored man gets a good break up here. I should know cause I'm from Clarksdale, Mississippi, right in the middle of the Mississippi Delta and KKK country." the man replied.

"You and your family have any place to stay?"

Mr. Elmore told him he didn't because he didn't know anybody outside his little town in Mississippi. He went on to tell him why he left everything and everybody behind. The farm he had lived on was owned by the descendants of the slave-owning plantation Sweetwater Oaks family, the Butler's. While most folks thought the Civil War had ended in 1865, they couldn't have been more wrong. For a brief period just after "the surrender", the Republican party controlled the Mississippi State House and encouraged free Colored men to run for office. Things got a lot better for Colored folks in the post-Civil War South. The Ku Klux Klan was conceived and founded, and free Colored men and white Republicans became fair game for the hooded cowards, with many beaten and hanged just because they were Republicans and Colored. Mr. Elmore went on to tell his story, one not unique to just him. Life on the plantation was just like in Feudal era England when the Lord of the Manor could "have his way" with any woman living on his property.

In the South, men from the big house would seduce or just kidnap young Colored girls and then gang rapes them. No white sheriff would even investigate such a charge by a Colored girl against a white property owner. Hell, it was a coming of age ritual to bust your cherry on a Colored tenant farmer's young daughter. Mr. Elmore continued to tell that three days before, he had stopped by his baby sister's to see if see needed anything from the store. When he walked into the front room, he saw his sister tied up to a chair and gagged. At first, he thought she had been robbed but what could anyone steal from a poor Colored dirt farmer's tenant house? Just then, he heard a cry from the bedroom room. As he opened the door, he saw the bare white ass of the plantation owner's son raping his niece. Her hands were bound to the frame of the Sears and Roebuck iron bed as were her feet. Something snapped inside Mr. Elmore. A lifetime of abuse by the white power structure in rural Mississippi had been pent up for far too long.

Having worked with his back and hands all his life, Mr. Elmore was strong for his size. The sight of his precious niece being raped at the age of 13 and fueled by the humiliating status of a Colored man in Mississippi in the 20's and 30's, all his pent-up rage exploded. That white boy was about to get a Saturday night juke joint ass whooping. Mr. Elmore picked the boy up and threw him across the room. The boy's pants were down around his knees and, strangely enough, his penis appeared not to be ready for any further sexual activities. Mr. Elmore wore hard toed Red Wing work boots, and although he had never played football, he seemed to land a perfect drop kick squarely in the assailant's nuts. A cry erupted from the boy that would raise the dead. Mr. Elmore proceeded to punch, hit and slap him until the kid had almost passed out. He continued to pound his little ass until both of the punk's eyes were almost swollen shut, and his lips were bleeding profusely. The boy staggered up and limped out to his pickup truck. Mr. Elmore followed him out and got to the truck first and snatched his keys away before delivering one more kick in the ass to the sobbing little excuse for a boy. He went back inside, untied his sister and niece, kissed them both and told them, he, his wife and son would be leaving Inverness and not coming back. His sister gave him a kiss and a hug, some ham and biscuits for the road and $17, all she had to her name. "Go," She told him "and don't look back. We will always love you."

Mr. Elmore drove straight home and told his wife the story. She said,

"I can be ready to go in 5 minutes. I don't care where we go as long as its north of the Mississippi Delta."

His story moved the ole man. He told Mr. Elmore all his children were grown up, and he and his wife had plenty of room for them until he got back on his feet. As they were preparing to leave, he turned to Mr. Elmore and said, "Did you work on tractors and farm equipment down on the farm?"

"I shore did, anything with a motor in it, I can fix."

"Well, this is a blessed day for you and your family. I'm a union steward at Caterpillar Company. If you don't mind working for $1.50 an hour, I can get you to work in a day or two."

Mr. Elmore couldn't believe his ears. Only less than ten minutes ago, he was out of gas, out of ham and biscuits and had no idea what he was going do for money or where his family would spend the night. They had been praying for a miracle since leaving Mississippi. First, the prayer was" Dear Lord, please helps us get out of Mississippi and Tennessee." The last day's prayer was "Dear Lord just show us the way to a better life." Now Mr. Ellis is talking about a job making a $60 per week. He only made $ 3.00 a week working six days a week, sunup till sundown down on the farm. Oh, and let's not forget fall hog killing bounty where he got to keep the chitin, balls, and feet after feeding their hogs all summer. None of the ham or ribs cause it went up to the Big House for the white folks and the house "n....r"s. And now the Good Lord had blessed him and his family with a guardian angel, Mr. Sam Ellis. It was almost like Harriet Tubman was looking down from Heaven over them as they traveled the latest version of the "underground railroad".

James was a teenager when they left Mississippi. But his Mamma had told him the story many times just in case he had forgotten about that miraculous northern sojourn to Peoria. He knew but for the grace of God goes him. Just one generation out of the South and he had a college degree in engineering from Purdue thanks to a football scholarship, something unachievable in the South. And now he was a fresh new engineer at Caterpillar. His father was one the Peoria plant's line supervisors who Caterpillar sent all over the world to supervise Caterpillar operations. James had volunteered for the Alaska Highway project because of the project's strategic value but also he wanted to give something back to the Colored folks his family had left down on the farm.

Sgt. Park reported to James and said,

"Sir, all the operators are here and ready to assist you,"

"Thank you, Sgt. Park, but I am a civilian, so there is no need to salute me or address me as Sir. Just call me Jim."

As Jim and two mechanics were preparing to start, Jim thought it would be nice to chat with the troops.

"I was born in Inverness, Mississippi in the Mississippi Delta, but my family moved to Peoria, Illinois back in the early 1930s. Is anybody from my neck of the woods? Only Aaron raised his hand.

"I am from Wren, Mississippi. That's just below Memphis and Tupelo, a ways from the Delta. My boss man, Mr. Davis, once went over to Greenwood. He said they were more stores downtown than any place he had ever seen, three movie houses, and a bunch of cafes like where my girlfriend Rose works in Chicago."

Jim could readily see Sgt. Park had potential like his Dad.

The men worked until the chow hall was open when Jim dismissed the platoon for the day. The rumor mill was spreading around the notion that tonight was steak night, so everybody raced over to get in line first. They moved down the chow line pass the white loaf bread, Sailor Boy crackers, and potatoes (they always had taters cooked some way). The men craned their necks to see the T-bone steaks on the line (#2 rule of rumor mills was the story gets better the more times folk retold it). When the men got to the meat station, the cook slapped some flat greasy pressed together piece of meat called Spam on their mess kits. The cook told them that this was a big treat in Hawaii. Before anyone could bitch about the food, Sgt. Park preempted them by telling all the guys,

"If this chow ain't to your liking, I'm sure the cooks could fry up some fat back and chitlins for you next time, maybe throw in some grits on the side."

Not another word was said about the food ever again, thank you very much. The ole mess sergeant just smiled knowing this sergeant's platoon would be fed well as long as he was in charge.

Everyone went back to the tents for the night. The CO had given the platoon leaders direct orders not to allow any of the Colored men off the airfield to go to the bars easily seen from their site. He said the white troops were being allowed to leave but had to be back at midnight. Captain Taylor told them,

"The reason the Colored units are restricted to garrison is the locals don't want any Colored folks mixing with the Eskimos or heaven forbid any white women. The local bars and cafes have signs in the windows that say

"No dogs, Eskimos, or "n....r"s allowed."

We may be 5,000 miles from Camp Shelby, but the attitude is about the same as down South.

Aaron decided not to tell his platoon anything more than no one is allowed off the field.

Aaron's bed check at 2200 hours discovered two men missing, his two New Orleans City Colored boys. These two were cut from a different bolt of cloth than the country Colored troops. God only knows what type of trouble these two were in by now. The rest of the platoon seemed to have a moral compass that didn't prevent them from doing stupid and dishonest things, but they at least knew when they did bad things. They knew it was wrong and would rather die than having to tell their Mamma about their sinful deed.

This pair was like no one Aaron had ever known, but he was sure he wouldn't hang out with their kind after the war.

Aaron had no option but report the infraction to Captain Taylor. He arrived at Base Ops to find the CO and the Ole Man in conference. Aaron made sure the CO knew he was outside and needed to see him. Captain Taylor visually acknowledged Aaron's presence.After a few minutes, Aaron was motioned into the Ole Man's office if you call a wood desk and a barrel for a seat an office. These old Army soldiers sure knew how to make do with what little they had. As Aaron walked in he came to attention and saluted as he said,

"Sirs, Sgt. Park reporting the results of the 2200 hour bed check (that's 10 PM National Guard and civilian time). I regret to report two of my men failed to report to the tent at 2200 hours as required. I am afraid they are off the airfield and in town. These two are from New Orleans and have been eyeing the bar just across the road. Their names are…."

Captain Taylor interrupted Aaron and said,

"Privates Cornelius and Brandon, right."

Aaron was embarrassed and stunned.

"How could the CO have known before me? I just found out. His head was spinning. Damn them fancy city "n....r"s. They ain't been anything but trouble since Shelby. I had hoped they would come around, but something was missing inside of them. Not the kind of soldier you wanted to be in a foxhole in battle. I'm gonna lose my stripes, maybe court-martialed. Damn, things are going from bad to worse."

Sgt. Park managed to regain his composure in time to stammer a pre-literate noise that could have been interrupted as, "Yes Sir," Aaron stammered nervously.

"Relax, Sgt. Park. The MPs have been picking up Colored soldiers all over town. You, however, are the only platoon leader in the three Colored Regiments to notice some of your men were missing. Things are out of hand now. The reason we knew Privates Cornelius and Brandon were missing from your platoon was due to a call from Fairbanks PD. It seems they found a poker game in the back of a bar, joined in and were caught cheating. Private Brandon pulled a knife out and was shot dead. Private Cornelius tried to take the gun away, was shot and also killed. All the witness conferred with the story. One of the players remarked,

"Ain't that just like an "n....r" to bring a knife to a gun fight!"

At any rate, the civilian portion of the case is closed. You will need to provide short statements reflecting the fact the soldiers in your platoon were briefed not to leave the airfield and the deceased soldiers were found missing at 2200 hours. That statement should close our case. Any questions, Sarge?"

"Sir, should I wake the platoon to tell them about the loss tonight or wait until morning?"

"Sarge, you have excellent judgment. I sure you will do and say the right thing."

Aaron returned to find most everyone was still awake. The confluence of poor field sanitation concerning mess kit cleaning at the lunch meal and an overactive rumor mill had more than half of the platoon attending to problems of the stomach. The remaining half were speculating where their two fancy city friends had gone. The mess kit fiasco was leading the race since multiple trips were needed to deal with a bad case of food poisoning. However, Aaron decided this was as good a time as ever to report the fate of the New Orleans duo.

"Men, I need your attention, please. I can see some of you that failed to clean out your mess kit properly are paying the price. I don't believe I need to cover mess kit cleaning, but I will. There are three cans, the first is filled with hot soapy water, the next can is for the first rinse, and a third can is for the final rinse. Do this every time you use your mess kit, and you will not get sick. The medics said you all will live, but tomorrow you will need to drink a lot of water.

The next thing I need to tell you is Privates Cornelius, and Brandon failed to report for the 2200 hour bed check. I reported this to the CO. Captain Taylor, and the Ole Man were talking when I got to Base Ops. They told me a lot of Colored soldiers disobeyed the Ole Man's order not to leave the airfield and were being picked up by the Fairbanks Police Department and our MPs. As all of you know, Cornelius and Brandon came from a far different background than most of us Colored country folks, and they loved to gamble. What you didn't know was that the way they won all of your pay was by cheating. But tonight they cheated some locals at a downtown bar, got caught and killed when Brandon pulled a knife. Cornelius tried to take the gun away and was killed too. The Bible says you reap what you sow, but they didn't need killing. The case is closed. There's a lesson for us. Stay out of town."

CHAPTER 5

CONSTRUCTION BEGINS

After days of preparation and modification of the equipment for extreme cold weather operation, the 95th Colored Engineer Regiment was ready to roll out and begin what was to be a yearlong project. Already some of their new equipment had been transferred to the white units over the objections of the CO, the Ole Man, and Jim Elmore, leaving the 95th with nothing but junk. This action only foretold events that would plague the unit for the rest of the project. Aaron thought to himself,

"Just like in Mississippi, the white man gets the fried chicken breast, and the "n....r" gets the ole cold tater to eat outside on the back porch."

With what equipment they had, the 95th moved out to their assigned location to set up camp. The quartermaster section had issued the platoon two tents, with four gasoline fueled stoves and one wood burning heater per tent.

The first camp was set up 140 miles east of Fairbanks with the notion that two teams would clear land and build bridges until they met. Then would move 40 to 50 miles and do it again until the road was complete. Aaron thought at least the weather had taken a turn for the better. The weather was above freezing now and the sun was melting the ice and snow, which as it turned out, to be a short-lived celebration.

Naturally, the white regiments got the task of improving the old road to Delta with the best equipment while the Colored 95th had to break new ground through tundra, muskeg, snow drifts, and creeks. The first week saw what came to be known as breakup. Aaron thought this was a damn good name for this God forsaken land. Everything was breaking up alright; ice, creeks, equipment and his back. Aaron hadn't had a letter from Rose in weeks but not because she didn't write. Their pie-eyed puppy love promises to write every day had hit the reality on both ends. However, Aaron had received a big bundle of letters from Rose in which she acknowledged she had gotten his letters. Most were just things about her life at home and how much she missed and loved him. He kept all the letters so he could read them over and over when he had a free minute.

The warmer weather had caused the road to turn into a quagmire of slurry mud. One morning Aaron had an idea. He climbed upon the biggest Caterpillar they had and proceeded to push the mud off to the side of the road instead of down the rough cut path. He cut trenches on both sides of the road with the blade and began pushing the mud over the side. This new technique started a flow of the water drying the road up faster than any time before. The rest of the dozer operators followed suit and started emulating their Sergeant. Sgt. Park' men were heard saying,

"That Sgt. Park is one smart Colored man."

The platoon made more progress that day than any other platoon in the company. But the Alaskan spring had more surprises in store for the 95th. Some of the ground weren't dirt, but this floating bed of grass called muskeg. Some of the men from the bayou country said they had the same thing down home, but they had never seen it frozen. As the days rolled on, the weather got warmer, and the more of this muskeg they found. After sinking a bulldozer so deep they couldn't get it out, the decision was made not to try to follow the survey team's markers but build around the muskeg. Aaron and the Co's kept this little secret because the white engineers weren't about to take no advice from a bunch of cotton patch Colored engineers. No one wanted the Colored units up in Alaska most especially General Simon B. Jefferson of Alaska Command. The General had descended from fine Southern landed gentry' antebellum lineage, having several Confederate high ranking officers listed in the family Bible. He had told the Washington War Department he believed Colored troops would be good only for pick and shovel work and should be kept out of the local villages to avoid any race mixing.

The next few days, good progress was being made until the invasion of the mosquitoes, flies, and other unidentified flying pests or UFPs. They came out of nowhere with little warning in large black swarms so thick you could barely see through the cloud. The lead dozer operator was the first one to be hit. The driver yelled so loud that everyone ran to see what prompted him to jump off the dozer. The dozer was still moving as the operator swung his arms around wildly. All eyes were focused on the operator, so they didn't see the black cloud of bugs descending on them, but that oversight was soon to be rectified. As soon as the men got the wild man on the ground, and the mosquitoes started to bit them, every last one of them was running, yelling or rolling on the muddy ground. The one that took off running learned a valuable lesson that day; your feet on the ground will not out run something flying in the air. The ones that were rolling around on the ground soon discovered when as soon as they were covered with mud, the biting stopped. It was a welcome relief for a situation that would be with them until the snow started to fall. A couple of South Mississippi boys had a solution for the muddy roads. They were from pine tree timber country and had to log into the spring when the ground was wet. The logs made the logging roads muddy just like the melting ground did in Alaska. Down South, they would cut small unmarketable pine trees 12-15 feet long and lay them down side by side across the road. This method called a corduroy road allowed all but the heaviest equipment to move over the road without getting stuck. In Alaska and western Canada, no shortage existed of useless sticks of trash wood pretending to be timber to use for road improvement. Since the white engineer's Regiment had been re-assigned over half of the Colored Regiment's equipment, ample manpower was available to cut and drag trees for road stabilizing purposes. This method saved the bulldozer operators time and fuel because the task of removing stumps was much easier than pushing over trees. Aaron's method of removing the slurry from the road to combat the permafrost issue had put Aaron's platoon as well as the rest of Captain Taylor's company in first place on the project.

When word of the pace of the 95th Colored Regiment's construction progress reached General Jefferson's staff, all hell broke loose. How these stupid country cotton patch Colored troops could be beating the white regiments was a situation not to be tolerated. Hell, they had stripped the units of all the best equipment and left them with the trashiest dozers and trucks. Something must be done to slow these Colored regiments down. The General was more concerned with his stubborn racialist mindset than protecting the

United States from a Jap attack. So a staff visit to the 95th Regimental HQ was planned in the next few weeks.

Back at the 95th's camp, the living conditions were harsh. After bitching about having to sleep on hay straw like a farm animal on the trip from the port, Aaron, and his men would give their left arm for a truckload of straw. Until they collected enough K-Rat boxes and scraps of wood from shipping crates to cover the ground in the tents, they had to sleep on the ground in the mud. The unit had not seen a hot meal for weeks, even though, a plan to bring hot chow up once a day had been scheduled. The mess truck made the trip from the main camp once but got stuck in the mud the next three days, so the run was on hold. The good news was they had all the K-Rats they wanted. Of course, if you ever had to eat one of these canned wonders, you know why not many would care to have a couple of boxes in reserve. Aaron had asked the CO about mail call since no letters had arrived out since they left Fairbanks. The mail was on the mess truck, and as soon as the road dried enough for the hot chow delivery, mail would be delivered, Aaron was told.

CHAPTER 6

TRAGEDY STRIKES THE 95TH

Road construction was a dangerous situation in a good climate. But up in Alaska, the weather, bugs mud, ice, and fatigue all joined forces to ensure you were working in the most accident prone environment imaginable. Every day someone bruised or cut parts of their body, but the unit medic was properly trained to treat such injuries. The unspoken concern was a more serious injury would have to be treated in the main camp, now over 90 miles away. The medical staff might as well be in Washington. 90 miles in the Alaskan spring on these muddy sometimes impassable roads was a death nail for a major injury. I guess that's the best they could do, but it seemed like another ole cold tater situation to the already abused Colored members of the 95th.

As fate would have it, the next day one of the men was walking along the side of a two and a half ton truck that been stuck in the mud when he tripped and fell under the tires. The driver had no way to know that he was about to run over his friend, so he drove right over him. People were waving and making hand gestures to try and stop him but to no avail. The rear dual mud grip tires rolled right over the poor soul's back. The troops closest to the accident said they heard a loud crack presuming it was the sound of his back breaking. His face was buried deep in the mud, and he had to be at least rolled over if he was to breathe. The medic was already on the way as the first men on the scène arrived and rolled him over. Once the mud had been cleared from of his mouth and nose, the medic administered a dose of morphine to ease the pain. The man was barely breathing, and his heart rate and pulse was very weak. Somebody had the presence of mind to find a couple of boards to use as support for his broken back. The medic said internal injuries were likely but with what he had to work with he had no way of knowing. This man had to reach the main camp and soon.

Captain Taylor knew there was only one man that had the skill and resourcefulness to save this trooper, Sergeant Park. Without saying a word to Aaron, only looking in his direction, the mission was a go.

"Yes, Sir Captain. I'll get this man to the field hospital."

For this situation, only one vehicle in the Army inventory would suffice; the Jeep 5/4 ton (or 1 and ¼ ton) transport. This truck sported with a 5000-pound winch, a covered cab and a 150-foot reel of wire cable. Aaron loaded some dead men, which were devices used to anchor into the ground so the hook on the winch cable can be attached, an ax, flashlights, three sleeping bags and, of course, the medic and patient. All of were loaded up in less than 3 minutes. Since Aaron thought of himself last if at all, Captain Taylor handed him several boxes of K-Rats and several canteens of water. He also gave him his Zippo lighter, a gift from his father, in case a fire needed to be built along the way.

Captain Taylor's final words before Aaron's departure was,

"Sgt. Park, no one at the hospital knows you are coming so give them this note spelling out what had happened. Drive fast but safe. You won't help anyone if you wreck and kill all three of you. Remember Rose is waiting for your return. Godspeed young man."

As Aaron pulled out on the muddy road, he could see all the men waving goodbye. The CO sure went for the jugular when he mentioned Rose. Aaron had only mentioned her once, and he thought. ***"How does that white man remember all that stuff?"***

Aaron turned around and told the medic to give him all the morphine he could because this wasn't going to be a pleasant trip. The road was horrible and only a few of hours of daylight were left. Driving at night in the cold will be a challenge, and Aaron hoped he could make it the 90 miles before sunset. At least for 40 miles he won't have to worry about oncoming traffic because this little stretch of mud road belonged to the 95th. As Aaron had expected, the road was muddy, but the drainage technique he had pioneered had dried the road up considerably since he had last traveled this section. Thank God he caught a break at last. He made good travel time until he reached the end of his unit's segment. He had been on the road less than two hours and was half way to the hospital. But the further he drove on the other regiment' segment, the worst the road became and the slower he had to drive.

"How's the patient doing? We are halfway, but the going will be slower for a while."

The medic said he was holding his own, but his pulse and blood pressure was in decline. The medic was afraid to give him more morphine unless the pain became unbearable. Aaron was driving faster than he had ever driven on a road like this one, and just when things were looking positive, a truck came into sight. Where that truck could be going at this time of day, was beyond Aaron. Both trucks flashed their headlights and signaled for each other to move over. The situation was rapidly becoming a standoff. Aaron tried to move over but kept sliding back into the center of the road due to the ruts made by big truck tires. The larger two and a half ton truck wasn't even trying to move, so Aaron just stopped in the middle of the road. The truck stopped, and a very angry white driver jumped out and raced toward Aaron. Aaron tried to tell him about the injured man's need for medical attention. But the white redneck driver wasn't going to listen to some cotton patch "n....r" tell him how to drive.

"Get your black ass out of my way or I will run you over. What are you even doing on this stretch of road? This road belongs to a white engineer regiment. No "n....r"s are allowed. Do you understands me, boy?

Aaron was trying hard just to cool this situation off, so he said the white man,

"Yes Sir, Mister Bossman. I knows I ain't got no right to bees on a white man road, but my white CO done sent me to the main camp on account of a dying soldier. I sure would be grateful ifin you could help a poor ole "n....r" out, kind sir."

"All right God Damnit, but just this once. Stay where you are, and I will go around you."

"Thanks you Mister thanks you."

The truck pulled over on the side of the road and flew pass
Aaron kicking up mud as high as you could see. Muddy water
immediately covered the windshield and came in the truck; Aaron
took out of the canteens out and cleaned the windows. As he got back
into the truck, he said to himself,

> ***"Fu........g redneck white mother....er, one day it will be
> my turn."***

After another hour of driving at speeds beyond the capacity
of the muddy pioneer grade road, Aaron was just beginning to have
some hope they would make it to camp and the hospital before dark.
The headlights were covered with mud, and the roadbed was shaded
by the many tall spruce trees and the angle of the Alaskan sunset.
He was driving on pure instinct when the Jeep bounced up off the
road, went airborne and came to land on its side. Aaron was thrown
out into the mud on the side of the road. As he rose, dazed from the
accident, he looked back up the road and saw a big spruce tree stump
in the middle of the road. Aaron surmised he had hit the tree truck
with his left front tire, and that was what sent him airborne. He ran
over to the overturned Jeep hoping his passengers were unhurt. To
his great relief, he found the medic holding the gravely injured soldier
tight as he could. Blood was pouring down from the medic's head,
but he was conscience.

"Doc, you okay? What about the private? Will he make it?"

"Yes, but you need to get this Jeep upright and back on the
road. Do you need my help?"

Aaron told him to stay in the covered truck. After a second look, the truck hadn't completely turned over and was leaning just on its side.

"No, you take care of the patient, and I will use the dead men and winch to right the truck. You both should be fine inside."

Aaron worked furiously to try to beat the fading daylight. Bug and flies were eating him alive, but nothing would keep him from completing the mission. Damn, he thought to himself,

"Just a few months ago, I was milking cows, killing hogs, chopping cotton and sweating my Colored ass off in Mississippi. Now I'm worried about saving a man's life I barely know and completing the mission. What's this Army done to me?"

With the Jeep back on the road, the trip to camp continued. Before they got to camp, the sun finally settled behind the mountains. With the loss of the sun, the blackest, darkest coldest night Aaron had ever seen began. He had no idea how far the camp was but according to his odometer, he had driven about 81 miles. No one knew exactly how far the camp was. It could be 5 minutes away or 45 minutes away. Now his night time visibility was near zero. Aaron had to slow down because another accident like before would surely mean death for his trooper.

"Doc, how's the patient? I believe we are only a few miles away, but I can't see shit and I'm afraid I will wreck again."

"Sergeant, just do your best. He still has a weak pulse, but he can't last much longer. And Sarge, no one could have done it better."

Aaron thanked the Doc and continued to press on. Just when he thought he would never make it to camp, an MP checkpoint came into sight.

"Halt and identify yourself!"

"Sergeant Park, 95th Colored Engineer Regiment with an injured man for the hospital, Sir'"

Aaron handed the MP the note from Captain Taylor. The MP read the note and said to Aaron.

"Is Captain Taylor your CO, Sarge?"

"Yes sir, he sure is. A fine man, if I might say so."

"You're a lucky man. Captain Taylor was our CO before he volunteered to command one of the Colored Regiments. No one could figure out why. Most consider the job of commanding a Colored unit a career killer. Consider yourself fortunate. Follow me to the hospital."

That big Red Cross looked mighty good as they approached the front of the medical tent. The MP had sent his runner ahead to alert the staff. Before Aaron could even stop the Jeep, Doctors and nurses were inside of the Jeep moving the injured trooper to surgery. The head nurse had read the note from the CO and turned to Aaron.

"Your CO said you were the best man he had, and you left the 95th camp four and a half hours ago. Is that right?"

Aaron thought he was in trouble. It was just that ole slave thinking coming out. Down on the farm, if something was busted; it must have been the "n....r" 's fault. Aaron was about to apologize for being late when the nurse called the Doctor.

"Yes Sir, I did but we had a little wreck on account of the dark and a stump in the road. I got the truck upright and back on the road as soon as I could."

"Well, Sarge, which makes this trip even more amazing. All our drivers have been telling the Ole Man the trip takes all day. You drove it in at least half of the trip in the dark, had a wreck and still made it here in just over four hours. Your friend is in surgery. He has broken back and some internal injuries. If you had been fifteen minutes later, he would have died. Good job, Sarge. Now you and the medic need to be checked. Then we get you a hot shower, some hot food, and a bed in the hospital for the night for observation. How's that sound?" "Great, just great," Aaron said.

THE TRIP BACK TO CAMP

Aaron found his way over to the mess tent early the next morning. He knew he was in enemy territory (white Engineer Regiment's land) and needed to keep a low profile. Just as he poked his head into the mess hall's back door, the mess sergeant came over and said.

"Well, if it's not the pony express of 5/4 drivers sneaking in the back door. I remember you from Ladd Field when you shut up your men when they started bitching about the chow in Fairbanks. I told myself I would take care of your men if I had a chance. The word's all over camp how fast you drove your injured man here. That was damn impressive, Sergeant Park."

The first thing you learn in the Army was the most important men in the unit were the Ole Man, XO, pay clerk, mess sergeant, and motor pool sergeant; not necessarily in that order. The ole mess cook had a big bundle of mail for the unit that had accumulated over the last few weeks. The ole Sarge had packed some hot chow in metal containers with enough food to feed his whole regiment. The early morning baking crew had even baked a big sheet cake with icing for the guys. An army moves on its belly, and this axiom was especially true for Southern Colored troops. As Aaron talked to the mess cook, he discovered he was from Chicago. He and Aaron promised they would keep in touch after the war since both had plans to return to Chi-Town.

With the 5/4 loaded up with goodies for the men, Aaron, and the Doc left for the 95th's camp. The head nurse had given Aaron a sealed envelope for Captain Taylor and told him all was being done for his friend. He was stronger but would not ever be returning to the unit. He would be transferred to Fairbanks for better treatment. Both Aaron and Doc agreed last night's sleep was the best sleep they had had since leaving Port of Valdez.

The trip back to camp was uneventful, and they made good travel time. The sun was out; the temperature was in the high forties and no stupid redneck truck driver to spoil the day. They arrived at the 95th's camp just after noon. Aaron assigned one of the men to guard the truck. He could make Captain Taylor aware of the situation concerning his man, mail call, and the hot (they hoped was still at least warm) chow. He reported to his CO.

"Sergeant Park reporting back from the main camp, Sir. The nurse told me to give this to you. I also have mail and hot chow."

"Stand at ease, Sergeant Park."

The CO read the note from the base hospital Commander. The Doctor explained Aaron had made better time than any of their men had during good driving conditions. He further explained had it not been for Sergeant Park' skills at driving under such horrid conditions; the injured man surely would have died.

"Well, Sarge, you did a fine job. We won't know for several days what's the extent of his injuries are, but one thing is for sure, he would have been dead if not for you. Good job Trooper. Since you brought the goodies, you should be the one tell the men."

If they were such a thing as Mayor of Colored Camp, Aaron would have been a shoo-in. The food was amazingly still warm, and the sheet cake had made the journey without an accident. With mail, hot chow and cake, things were looking up for the 95th Colored Regiment. But, of course, unknown to them was the General Jefferson's staff visit heading for them early in the next week or two. God only knew what the Command had in store for them.

The troops' were told their friend had made it to the Camp Hospital. But the note the CO received revealed the grim prognosis. As the medic feared, internal injuries were far worse than could be handled at the Camp Hospital. The Colored soldier would only be treated in a native only section of the Fairbanks Hospital, depending on bed space. No beds were available, so all that could be done at camp was manage the decline and hope something opened up soon. The fact that plenty of beds were available in the white section made no difference to the Fairbanks Hospital staff.

CHAPTER 7

GENERAL JEFFERSON'S REVENGE

June 1942

The tally for completed road construction mileage was compiled for the first two months. To the chagrin of the Alaskan Command's staff, the 95th Colored Regiment was number one by a wide margin, so a visit was scheduled for the early part of the following week. A good staff knows what results their commander desires, so no orders had to given to draft a plan to slow the progress of the 95th. Since they had taken most of their good equipment and re-issued it to the white regiments, little more could be done to slow road construction. However, a temporary change of mission just might do the trick. A bridge needed to be built over the Sikanna Chief River in British Columbia, and the White engineer regiment said it couldn't be built in less than six weeks. The staffers at Alaska Command decided this would be the perfect diversion for the 95th. By assigning them the task of building the Sikanna Chief River Bridge, Jefferson's staff figured the cotton patch Southern "n....r"s would screw up the construction thus requiring the white regiment's help to salvage the project. The bridge construction without the right equipment would be back breaking hard dangerous work and according to most observers, a recipe for failure.

As scheduled, General Jefferson arrived at the main camp on Monday. He and his staff were briefed on the overall progress and each Regiment's sector of responsibility. When the 95th segment of the briefing began, Jefferson's boot licking Chief of Staff asked if the unit was up to the task.

"We've had reports of an unwarranted high rate of injuries and poor equipment maintenance in the 95th. We have concerns at HQ about the perception that Colored Regiments are being put at risk. What are your plans to correct this situation?" the Chief of Staff asked the Commander.

LTC Noble addressed the question gingerly since General Jefferson had a reputation as a racist. What he would like to tell him was HQ had done everything in its power to sabotage the Colored Regiments work. But being a good officer he decided to soften his reply.

"Sir, we are aware of the rate of injuries and have taken positive steps to reduce the risks on the job sites. On the troops off-cycle downtime, we have introduced safety classes to reinforce the training they received in Advanced Individual Training (AIT) in Chicago. This sort of work is new, but the men are adapting, Sir."

"I hope so LTC Noble. We received a report of a life-threatening injury last week. We understand this soldier broke his back and had to transported to the Camp Hospital. The report also states he was near death and is awaiting transfer to Fairbanks. We know this was a preventable accident, and the truck driver was at fault. Is that correct?"

"For the most part, Yes Sir. However, I wouldn't characterize the instance as driver error. Given the weather and road conditions, I don't believe the driver is responsible."

"God Damnit LTC Noble, we have looked at this at HQ and have determined the driver to be at fault. I want an Article 32 inquiry conducted immediately, and court marshal proceedings scheduled. Do you understand?'

"Yes Sir, I do understand."

What LTC Noble understood was this Colored soldier was about to be sent to prison for a long time for something he didn't do. The fact that the Ole Man wanted court marshal proceeding scheduled before the completion of the Article 32 investigation told him the outcome was pre-ordained. PVT Early would be guilty as charged just for being a member of the 95th Colored Regiment. Just good ole time-tested Southern white man justice. Yes, Sir, General Jefferson knew how to keep his "n....r"s in line. All that bullshit about putting Colored troops in the regular Army must have been some of the radical crap the President's wife Eleanor's doing according to the General.

The news had to be broken to PVT Early, the driver of the truck that ran over his friend. They had grown up together in Mississippi and knew each other family well. Pvt. Early even had eyes for George's little sister. He and George had hunted; fished, chopped cotton; cursed white men and everything else Colored men did in the South. The two admired Sergeant Park. Sarge had seemed to have risen above the rest of them, giving them some hope of a better life after the war. PVT Early had been in a deep depression over the accident and wondered how he was going to tell George's folks. He had to do it in person, but that wouldn't happen for a long time. All of the guys in the company told him it wasn't his fault, but the reassurance did little to relieve the pain he was feeling. The CO had informally put him on close quarter's observation, sort of a mild suicide watch.

The Ole Man and the CO arrived back at the camp the following day. The CO called platoon leaders meeting to brief them on the HQ Staff visit. Most was routine until the company platoon leaders learned about their new mission; construction of the Sikanna Chief River Bridge.

"Men, we have never built a bridge before but we had never built a road before a couple of months ago. We will approach this undertaking with all the skill and confidence we can muster. From what I saw of the plans, the river is a glacier fed swift running river. A minimum of three pilings will have to be set, and timber cut on site. We will have a five horsepower gasoline driven sawmill at our disposal operated by some locals. Most of the work will be by hand so prepare your men for a long hard work schedule. We will be running almost 20 hours a day so rest will be short. No one believes we can bring this project in on time, but I know you can do this. Let's show HQ how wrong they are about the 95th. Any questions? Sergeant Park, please remain behind. The rest of you are dismissed."

Aaron was puzzled. What had he done wrong? Aaron still hadn't shed the slave mentality of the ole South were everything wrong was blamed on the "n....r" boy. Just as his imagination was about to go into overdrive, Captain Taylor spoke up.

"Sergeant Park, you and I have to deliver some bad news to Pvt. Early. Headquarters decided the accident last week was due to operator error. Due to the severity and extent of the injury, a court marshal will be convened. An Article 32 investigation will be conducted, but HQ has already made their mind up. We have to tell Pvt. Early. There's something else I need to share but only if you give me your word not to tell anyone else."

What choice did Aaron have?

"Yes Sir, Captain Taylor, you have my word of honor."

A Mississippi "n....r" didn't have much in this ole world, but the Army had reinforced his faith in God and planted a sense of honor in his soul that would serve him a lifetime.

No damn white man can ever take one's honor away.

"Sgt Park, George's medical condition is far worse than I have led you and your men to believe. He had massive internal injuries as well as a broken back. His transfer to Fairbanks has been delayed because although space is available in the hospital, the staff refuses to put Pvt Jones in the whites' only section. The few beds assigned to Alaska natives were full. Before the Camp Hospital can transfer him, a bed must be available in the Native section. It's not right; it's not fair and one day I hope soon, white folks will look back on these days and wonder how their parents and grandparents could allow this to happen. However, this is today, and that's the lousy hand we have been dealt. You need to go and find Pvt. Early and report back here ASAP. Do you have any questions?"

Aaron replied "No Sir, but I don't have to tell you Pvt. Early is already down in the mouth about his best friend's accident. He already blames himself."

"I know Sarge. This decision is a shitty deal, but the Ole Man, and I pleaded Pvt. Early's case before the General. He was adamant about the court marshal. I have no other options. I will break the news to him."

Aaron saluted and left to find Pvt. Early. As usual, Pvt Early was working his heart out on the dozer. Aaron waved and caught his attention. He motioned for him to come over to him. As Pvt Early approached; he could see Sgt. Park' face was not his usual cheerful self. The first thing Pvt Early thought was George's condition.

*"**God help me Dear Lord, sweet Jesus. Please don't take George from his folks and me. I couldn't live with the notion I had killed my best friend."** Pvt Early thought as Aaron approached.*

"The CO wants to see us for a minute."

"What's this about? It's about George ain't it? He done gone and died. Oh, sweet Jesus, say it ain't so Sarge, say George ain't done passed!"

Aaron assured him George hadn't died. The CO had something else to talk to him about.

"Oh God, it's my Pappy down in Mississippi. He must have done passed. That's it ain't it?"

"Pvt Early, let the CO tell you before you go and kill off all your family and friends. I don't know what it's about."

Sgt Park had told a little white lie for the sake of his man. This news was going to be as bad as losing a loved one because he will most likely go to jail. Aaron couldn't shake the thought about the unfairness of the court marshal. A poor ole Southern Colored boy was about to be railroaded and sent to an Army prison for something he didn't mean do. Pvt Early had rather cut his arm off as hurt his long time buddy George. The outcome of a bunch of white folks judging a Colored boy from Mississippi would not be good. Aaron had seen it too many times down South before to have any hope for Pvt. Early.

As the two walked into the CO's quarters, he realized the Ole Man was there. "Sir, Sgt. Park and Pvt. Early reporting as ordered."

"Pvt Early, there's no easy way to say this, but HQ is convening a court marshal hearing for you on the charge of willful misconduct that resulted in the injury of a US soldier. Pvt. Jones's permanent disability condition is the result of unlawful and willful disregard for the health and safety of the surrounding personnel. You will be formally charged as soon as the Article 32 investigation is complete. The court marshal proceeding will be set at HQ sometime next month. You will not be jailed, but you are restricted to your duties and your quarters. You are looking at 15 years in military prison. Do you understand the charges?" Captain Taylor said.

"I don't know sir. I was just driving, and George was walking beside me. The sun was in my eyes, and the windshield was muddy likes it always is. I didn't mean to hurt my best friend. I swear it, Sir." He pleaded.

"I am truly sorry, Pvt. Early. You will have a JAG lawyer assigned to your case. We will give you all the support we can. Do you have any questions?" The CO said to Pvt. Early.

"No Sir."

"Dismissed." the Captain said. Aaron could see Pvt. Early's legs were weakening so he gave him a hand getting out of the tent.

CHAPTER 8

1ST CAUSALITY OF THE ALASKA INVASION

June 3, 1942

Aaron had briefed the platoon on Early's charges. He made sure their concern for Early overwhelmed the injustice of the pending court marshal. The next day at breakfast everyone including PVT Early looked to be in good spirits. Too damn good, Aaron thought for someone facing a US Army court marshal. Aaron walked over to Pvt. Early and said,

"You know, we all are pulling for you so don't get all down in the mouth over this situation."

Pvt Early looked at his beloved and respected Sergeant and said in an eerily calm tone,

"Sarge, I prayed on it, and the Lord showed me the way to salvation. I am fine with the world. Please don't worry about me."

Aaron was puzzled at his choice of words but decided Early's come to Jesus conversation with the Lord had given him some internal solace and peace.

On some desolate cold beach in the far Aleutian Islands of Attu, Jap troops were invading American soil. For the first time since the war of 1812, foreign troops were attacking the US on the ground. The war had come to Alaska, and the Alaskan-Canadian Highway project would suddenly jump to the top of the War Department's list of priorities. The news traveled slow and won't reach the Camp HQ for two days. By the time the camp heard about the invasion, the War Department was already ramping up to reinforce the Engineer Regiments with more and better equipment. Unknown to the 95th, life was about to get even harsher. The equipment shipment would take weeks to arrive but pick and ax work could pick up immediately.

Aaron was supervising his men as usual. Trees were being felled and snaked by truck or dozer to reinforce the permafrost sections of the new road. Things were going about as peaceful as it could when he heard a great deal of shouting up the road. He ran as fast as he could up the road toward the commotion when he saw the genesis of the disturbance.

Right in the middle of the road was Pvt. Early, standing in front of his unmanned bulldozer that was creeping toward him at a snail's pace. Pvt Early had left his dozer in a lower forward gear, climbed down and had taken a position in front of the left track. People were running toward him, others were yelling, and some were running to get the Doc. Aaron ran harder than he knew even possible but to no avail. Just as he got close enough to see Early's face, the tracks consumed his whole body. Not one scream or call for help was heard. The big earth mover slowing rolled over the poor boy body as he just smiled and closed his eyes for the last time. Death would have been quick but not painless. Aaron sent a runner to inform the CO as he and the whole platoon waited for what seemed an eternity for the dozer to clear his broken, lifeless body. One of the men had jumped on the bulldozer to try to stop the carnage but arrived too late. Nothing could be done for Pvt. Benjamin Early, US Army from Houston, Mississippi. The son of Robert and Bessie Early would shortly receive a telegram from the War Department which always started,

> ### *"The War Department regrets to inform you..."*

PVT Benjamin Early was mostly likely the first causality of the Aleutian Island Campaign, killed not by a Jap soldier but by racism, shame, and guilt. General Jefferson now had his hands full with Japs on Alaskan soil to worry much about proving his outdated theorem about the inferiority of the Negros from the South. It was a good thing the General's mind was elsewhere but unfortunately too late for Early.

Aaron thought,

> ### *There must be a special section of Hell for mother....ers like Jefferson.*

A small memorial service was held for Pvt Early by the platoon. One of the men read passages from the Bible, and people got up to recite fond memories of the recently departed Ben Early. RIP, my friend, they said as they returned to the back breaking work at hand.

Captain Taylor assigned one of his men to transport the body to the HQ Camp Morgue. He gave the driver a sealed letter to be delivered to the Head Nurse or the Hospital Commander immediately upon arrival. On the front read in red letters, PLEASE OPEN IMMEDIATELY AND READ Captain Taylor Commanding.

The trip took five and a half hour that was better than the driver had expected. The twenty hours of sunlight per day had dried the road bed up over the past weeks that made driving faster and safer. Other than having a dead friend in the back, the driver enjoyed the break from the daily grind of road construction. All the mosquitoes and bugs stayed out of the cab by driving 35-45 mph. The cool 55-degree temperature was a welcome change, something he would brag about to his buddies for weeks to come. Not many Colored soldiers ever got to leave camp, so being picked was a treat. He wished his trip was for hot chow, something that didn't show up at Colored Camp very often, and not his friend death. It was a good thing the Ole Man and the Co didn't tell all the men about the railroad job the Command at HQ had in store for Early. Most just thought he was guilt ridden about hurting his best friend. Sometimes the truth is not the best policy when a bigger job is at hand. On June 6, 1942, nothing was more important to the war effort than linking the contiguous 48 states with Alaska.

The driver arrived ahead of schedule with the body and the letter from the CO. As he climbed out of the cab of the Jeep, an orderly greeted him.

"What brings the 95th to HQ? You fellers must be out of chow?"

"No sir, I'm afraid we done had us a death. One our friends that drove the dozer fell off and got runned over. He was killed him as we watched." The driver told the orderly.

"My CO said I was to give this to the Big Doc or the nurse first off."

The driver showed the orderly the letter that he read.

"Come with me and I'll help you find one of them. This letter looks important."

Pretty soon, the two found the Hospital Commander, a Full Bird Colonel that looked old enough to have served in the Civil War, who took the letter, opened it and read it to himself.

"This contains the report on the death of Pvt. Benjamin Early, which I have determined his death to be in the line of duty. He had been despondent over the injury of his best friend who is in your care. I do not think this condition had any bearing on this accident. Please advise me of the status of Pvt. George Jones, the soldier with the broken back, in writing and don't let my driver speak to him. I had rather brief with the entire platoon at once on his condition rather than after the rumor mill. Please allow the driver to have chow and have him return to our Camp.

Thanks for your consideration,

Captain Taylor

Commanding"

When the driver returned, he had mail, a big box of cookies from the mess hall and a sealed letter from the Hospital Commander. Captain Taylor confirmed his worst fears. Pvt. George Jones had been transferred the day before to Fairbanks, but the delay had been costly. By the time he was admitted and sent to the operating room, his blood pressure was extremely low. The surgeons tried their best, but PVT. Jones died on the operating table. Maybe something could have been done had he been transferred the same day but the delay cost him his life. It's not right to draft someone into the Army, send him on a dangerous mission and then put white civilians ahead of him when he is dying. It was especially true of the outlaw bunch of sons of bitches running and living in Fairbanks. Captain Taylor decided the platoon had enough bad news in the last 24 hours. The news about the Aleutian invasion would be enough news for today. He decided to wait a couple of days before breaking the bad news about PVT Jones.

By the times the CO arrived at the platoon area, all the cookies had already been eaten, and the mail had been distributed. He addressed the men saying,

"Men, the war has come to Alaska. Yesterday morning an invasion force of 20,000 Japs invaded the Aleutian Island of Attu. Granted the island is 1500 miles from here, but Jap planes have bombed Dutch Harbor, a vital shipping port much closer to here. All military units are on the highest possible alert, and our project just got even more important. The brass thinks the Japs might be planning a leap frog type action up the chain with two invasion forces fighting at the same time. It's too early to speculate, but the invasion of the United States has begun. We have received no formal briefing by HQ on the exact status this enemy action will have on us but rest assured it will speed up the construction. Expect longer hours and harsher working conditions. I know all of you have in the guts and drive you will need for this task. Remember all your hard work is for all your loved ones at home. There is no more news on Pvt. Jones' status but as soon as I know something I will pass it along. Do any of you have any questions?"

Captain Taylor had considered saying let's do this for God and country, but both had let these Colored men down. He decided against the God and country party line and went the loved one's option. They all cared about their kinfolks back home.

CHAPTER 9

NOT ALL THREATS HAVE TWO LEGS

The first major change in routine was a perimeter patrol had to be posted each night at 2200 hours until 0700 hours the following morning. The biggest problem wasn't the slimmest of a chance of seeing a Jap. But encountering a hungry bear or wolf that was almost a sure bet at night. The bears especially had good noses and could smell food miles away. As many times as the troops had been told not to leave food out, the food was always in the reach of bears. The next big problem was only the Officers had weapons unless you classified K-Rats cans as lethal. The jury was still out on that issue. So instead of issuing weapons, the patrol was issued whistles. Sure, they were loud and obnoxious sounding, but something told the troops the bear still had the advantage and was still at the top of the food chain. At least the noise from the whistle stood a chance of scaring a wild bear off. The guys have been feeding some of the cute small black bears. The problem is all they were doing were making the bears less afraid of humans. And when the crap from K-Rats runs out, guess who would be on the menu, you.

The wolves were a bigger threat than the bears. They ran and attacked in packs. They could bring down a bull moose, kill and eat most of it in a few hours. The wolves didn't care if their prey was two or four legged, walked or ran; when the pack set its sights on you, you were supper. They also were silent hunters and very intelligent. An attack by a pack of wolves usually appeared to have been planned and not a random act. While two or more wolves were biting at a victim's extremities, one would zero in on the soft, vulnerable belly that housed the vital organs. This area was easy to rip opened with their razor-sharp canine teeth exposing vitamin rich organs like the liver. The person would still be alive while being eaten for many terrifying agonizing minutes before succumbing to blood loss. The small intestine would be eaten while the victim was still conscience as would large chunks of flesh from the arms and legs. You could kick, scream and try to run but as soon as the pack selected you for supper, you were a dead man walking. Wolves also, like bears, had a good sense of smell. The men worked hard long hours wearing the same clothes for weeks at a time. They only had a chance to bathe when a pond or creek was near, so the unit's collective body odor was beyond belief. A wolf pack could pick up the scent miles away and maneuver in and surround a person before they knew it. The attack would be swift and lethal. By the time the screams brought help, it would be all over. If there was an upside to the possibility of a bear or wolf attack was that no one dared to go to sleep on duty. Make it through the night, and you were off until 1500 hours the next day. The patrol was briefed on all the dangers. They were told the duty officer had a weapon and could come to their rescue if needed. That was a good plan on paper, but most of these officers held the Colored troops and their assignment in such contempt, they wouldn't lift a finger to save any of the patrols from an attack.

A month had gone by with the road construction project ahead of schedule. The Sikanna Chief River Bridge project had been put on hold. The Engineers had designed a temporary floating bridge plan that might suffice until the next spring if the winter delayed the construction. The camp had been moved again, and they were getting further and further from Camp HQ. The ever increasing remoteness of their camp was a good situation for the 95th. None of the HQ brass wanted to bounce up and down on the pioneer road, and most especially didn't want to get stuck in the middle of nowhere. You could bet their lily-white asses weren't going to get mud on their fancy spit-polished Cochran jump boots they wore around HQ. No sir, you could bet the farm on that. The 95th camp was now too far for the brass to drive from Fairbanks to the 95th and back in one day. You count on the fact that they weren't going camp out with a bunch of smelly Colored boys.

"Oh, the things we could do to them if they stayed overnight. A small turn on the tire valve stem core early in the morning could cause a flat tire many miles away from help. You could deflate the spare since none of them would bother to check the tire pressure. Any good mechanic could short out the fuel quantity gauge, remove most of the gas and ensure they would run out of fuel way down the road just in case the tire didn't go flat soon enough. And one of all time favorites was to put a small pin hole in the brake line so every time they pumped the brakes a little bit of brake fluid would escape through the pin hole. Those were just the surprises for the drive home. For the night's entertainment, bear baiting their tents would be a winner. With any luck, one of the brown bears would come into the tent and have his way with all those pricks. Of course, all the troops would come running observing all the safe workplace rules the HQ brass

had sent down to the letter. The soldiers all hoped they would arrive just in time to blow their whistles at the bear."

As they expected, no staff visits were planned. They didn't need any more incentive to build the road faster than for their kin folks, but keeping the brass out of their hair was icing on the cake. By now, the 95th had been issued more equipment but just like before the white regiment had first pick. What the 95th got was better than the equipment they had on hand before, so they made do. The nights were getting colder and on the first damp morning you could see a little bit of snow on the tops of the mountain.

One of the old sourdough Alaskans called it termination dust. He said that's when most folks start preparing for winter in earnest. Preparing for winter for Alaskans starts at breakup in the spring with gardens being prepared, planted, tended, and grown, and the bounty canned. Hay fields are planted for livestock's winter feed. Bear baiting spots are picked out and most important of all, the preparation for the fishing season. All species of salmon were good for something. You might store canned, smoked or dried salmon for future consumption. Your dog team needs protein during the cold winter months because hungry, weak dogs don't mush very well and dog salmon were plentiful. On a good salmon spawning creek or the Yukon River, a fish wheel or set net would yield enough fish for your family and dog team for nine or ten months. All of this preparation meant nothing to most of the men of the 95th. In the South on the very coldest night in winter; preparations meant bringing in the plants in off the Misses back porch at night. Hell, down South you could catch you some supper with a worm and bobber most any time of the year. Even when the fish weren't biting, your 22 caliber rimfire, Western Auto single shot rifle could be counted on to kill enough rabbits or squirrels to make a good stew fit for a King. Yes sir, there's something to be said for just getting up off your ass and catching or killing something for supper anytime a little hunger pain hits your belly. You could bet that same farm again K-Rats weren't high on the food pantry list. The only exception would have been if they had never eaten any of the horrific stuff.

Can't you just picture the scene in the little trapper's cabin in January. Snow outside piled up past the window sill, wind whipping up your back side at 50 mph, wolves howling, and you bring out some K-Rats you stole off an Army supply truck last summer. You had been telling your whole family how good these little cardboard boxes of cans were. You had filled your small daughter's head with tales of chocolate bars and jelly hidden inside those boxes that you had put in especially for his little angel. Yes, you could see it all now. You were about to be an even bigger hero in his wife and daughter's eyes. Hell after this feast, you just might get to put the girl to bed early so you and the misses could root around under the bed covers like the Eskimos did. Out of the blue, Realville sets in about the time the ole lady gulps down her first big bite of peas and ham. The daughter breaks the last of her baby teeth on the John Wayne Chocolate bars, and you find yourself outside hip deep in the snow with orders not to come back without something dead that has a face.

If there was one thing the supply sergeant didn't need to be worried about being stolen were K-Rations.

The pace of construction had picked up as the summer morphed into fall in the Yukon. The 95th was well into Canada by now, so the CO said. How they knew where they were was a mystery. All the trees and bugs looked and felt the same. A Yukon mosquito bit just like an Alaskan mosquito, and the Yukon mud was just as sticky and smelled just like that ole Alaskan mud. Those damn cardboard boxes of K-Rats didn't improve any when the 95th moved across the border, and the bears and wolves weren't any friendlier. After a couple of months of night patrols, the men got too lax with their duties. The Officers charged with night staff duty were just as lax and lazy. The men on night patrol hadn't seen any of the Officers except for Captain Taylor since the first week. You could say the 95th mission was a total success in battle since not one little slant-eyed yellow Jap had managed to breach the perimeter of the mighty 95th Colored Engineer Regiment.

One night just after the first dusting of snow had started to fall, Pvt. Willie Wilson of Wesson, Mississippi had the perimeter duty guarding the north sector of the encampment. He and all his buddies had forgotten all about the Japs. They still were afraid of bears and wolves. But except for a few daytime bear sighting, no predators had been encountered. Little did anyone know that a pack of wolves driven down from the mountain timberline by the snow had been stalking the night patrol for the last several days. Most of the time two or three men would gang up the fire and bullshit about the things GIs bullshit about in their spare time. But tonight Willie hadn't made his way over to the fire pit to join in yet. He had found him a big tree to squat down beside so he could look at the beautiful moon in the distant sky. The twenty hour days of daylight were gone until next spring and winter was coming. Willie thought to himself,

"Hell, they don't have a summer up here. The only day that even felt like a summer day was in July. We should have had a picnic to celebrate the Alaskan summer of 1942."

Willie was hoping to see what the sourdoughs called the "northern lights"; a spooky bunch of lights that danced across the sky, sometimes in color. The lights were a sight to see. Nothing like that ever happened in South Mississippi pine tree country unless you counted the fireflies. They were awfully pretty, but they couldn't hold a candle to them northern lights. They almost put you in a trance, letting your mind wander back to a more pleasant place and time. Willie had drifted off into a light sleep, a no-no for patrol duty. He was having a dream about his girlfriend back home. She sure was a pretty thing. Willie and Mae Bunch had been going together ever since they were in grammar school. Willie didn't make it pass the 8th grade, but that achievement was two grades ahead of his pappy. The thing Willie liked most about Mae was she didn't wear no drawers when they would sneak off together to Mr. Harry's hay barn. Mae had made a man out of Willie several years ago in that hot ass hay barn. He acted like he was an ole hand at the sex game, but Mae knew better. Seems Willie for the first few things in the barn with the gal with no drawers had finished before he got started if you know what I mean. But after several tries, Willie managed to please the worldly Mae Bunch as they rooted around on bales of Johnson grass hay.

Every one of these sexual encounters was replaying in Willie mind that night when something awoke him from his wet dream. He could smell a strange odor unlike any he had ever smelled. It was a musty damp, rotten meat sort of odor. The air around him became hot and moist and seemed to come from out of nowhere. He had been in a deeper sleep than he thought because it seemed he was having trouble waking up. An unexpected nip was felt in his ear from behind him. His eyes were still focusing when he saw in front of him, the biggest meanest most vicious creature he had ever laid eyes on. It was a gray wolf so big the wolf had to look down at him. The introduction was short and swift. Two pack members were stationed behind Willie as if awaiting the signal to commence the attack. Willie was petrified with fear, had no weapon and had forgotten his whistle. Willie was a dead man and supper for this pack. In the moonlit Yukon night, Willie made out three more sets of eyes, just waiting to pounce upon his poor body. Willie had been bitten by big dogs before and knew dog bites hurt, but he had no concept of what the last few minutes of his life were going to be like. As if on cue, the wolves attacked. First the two behind him started taking big chunks of flesh from out of his back and neck as the alpha male went for the belly. The big male's canine teeth tore through the outer shirt in mere seconds and were soon ripping the belly open like you would gut a fish. Willie cried out in pain, and sheer terror but no one came a running. It was a clear cold night and sound usually travels fast in clear conditions such as tonight. But the sad fact was if everyone had come running to help, Willie would have still died. The alpha male took a big bite out of Willie's liver and then started to eat his intestine. Willie's pain was beyond what any man should ever have to endure. The other two wolves moved in and started to eat as soon as the alpha male was finished. They took turns pulling out Willie's organs using their paws to break the organs out of the stomach cavity when mercifully, the loss of blood finally put poor Willie out of his misery. The feeding frenzy continued until almost all the flesh had been stripped from the bones. The stomach and chest cavity was cleaned out better than a union meat worker in the Chicago stockyard could do. The wolves ate the eyeballs and the ears. All soft tissue was eaten. The attack wasn't a personal thing for this pack. This sort of attack happened every few days all through the year.

By the time Willie was missed at chow the next morning, the pack had moved on was mostly likely fifteen to twenty miles away in areas no man could travel. Willie had told his buddies about the gal with no drawers and some of the sexual encounters he and Mae Bunch had shared. One of the men in the platoon said,

"I bet ole Willie done had himself a wet dream about that Mae. In my head, she sure is pretty and keeps me warm at night. Just you wait till he gets here. I'm gonna give him the red ass about the gal with no drawers."

But Willie never showed up after chow. Aaron notified the CO that a man was missing, and he had been on patrol duty the night before. A search party was quickly formed and sent out to his sector. The search didn't last long. Within a few minutes, a loud report from a whistle was heard, so everyone started running in the direction of the sound. As Aaron and the CO arrived, they saw the carnage of what once just a few hours before was Pvt. William Wilson of Wesson, Mississippi. The men that had arrived at the site earlier were throwing up and weeping uncontrollably. Never had anyone in their entire life ever seen anything close to the horrific sight. Captain Taylor ordered all the men back to camp except for Aaron and a runner. The CO sent the runner to Regimental HQ to report the death. The CO wrote a short but informative note to his boss.

"Man mauled, killed and eaten by a pack of wolves. The unit is in a panic. Please advise. A more detailed report will be coming. Captain Taylor."

"Get this to LTC Noble at Regimental HQ ASAP (as soon as possible) and await his reply.

"Sergeant Park, we are in uncharted waters now. I have no idea what this will do to the men. The sight is burned into my brain as I'm sure everyone else that saw it has it in their memory forever. I have not been in combat, but I can't imagine anything on the battlefield worst. We need to have a platoon meeting to sort this situation out. Go back to your men and do what you can until I hear back from Regiment HQ. Any questions?"

Aaron returned to his platoon. When he arrived, all the men were huddled up talking to each other. The men stopped talking and looked at their sergeant hoping he would have some consoling words to ease the horror they had just witnessed. Aaron had no idea what to say so he just spoke from the heart.

"Men, we all have lost a friend in the most terrible way any of us could imagine. When we get into combat, I am sure we will lose friends again but I pray to God none of us we ever have to see what saw this morning. I believe the best thing we can do is have a silent prayer for the soul of Willie Wilson. Please bow your head."

After a few minutes, Aaron said Amen and dismissed the troops. Today the Alcan Highway construction would have to wait for Willie Wilson's soul to leave.

CHAPTER 10

REVENGE FOR PRIVATE
WILLIE WILSON

Within an hour, LTC Noble was at the scene. The men could see this WW1 Army veteran of the Belgium trench warfare was taken back. He had a grave registration officer from the Regimental S-4 section to claim the body so Pvt. Wilson's remains could be removed from the company area. The sooner this task was accomplished, the better. The Ole Man knew something had to be done and done quickly. He had already sent a runner to HQ in Fairbanks to advise them of the situation. The Ole Man had been around the Army long enough to know it's easier to get forgiveness than permission especially if things turn out positive. He had informed the General's staff he was authorizing the rental of a plane, pilot, and sharpshooter to hunt down this pack and kill them. With the dispatch en route, LTC Noble and Captain Taylor set out to find a pilot to bring back the hides of the killer pack that had viciously taken the life of one of their men. The ride to the border would take most of the day, but he knew a small trading post just over the Alaskan-Canadian boundary where a bush plane was tied down. Everything in Alaska is for hire at a price, and money was no object on this mission. The men of the 95th needed to see wolf hides nailed on the wall before justice would be served. The truck that was carrying the Ole Man, the CO and driver rolled into the small trading post at about 2000 hours. As they had hoped, a yellow and black high wing airplane was tied down by a log cabin next to a dirt strip. A big steel container with a winged Pegasus emblem painted on the tank with the words ESSO in blue underneath. A red windsock fluttered in the night breeze against the backdrop of a full moon. The northern lights danced in the sky showing bands of color with a tip of the stream pointing down at the eastern end as if to point to the wicked pack they sought.

The Old Man and the CO walked inside to find what was most likely a nightly occurrence of drinking, gambling, and flirting with the barmaid. Now this gal wouldn't turn anybody's head most places with her ample belly and hips combined with some her questionable and infrequent bathing habits in Anchorage or Fairbanks. But at the Far North Trading Post, she was the belle of the ball. The two troopers found a table and settled down hoping for a meal and beer before calling it a night. By now their driver had joined them. After ordering moose burgers, fried potatoes, and beer, the CO asked the barmaid if they could rent a room for the night. After securing lodging, they asked her if the plane outside was for rent. The barmaid pointed to a tall well-girthed man with shoulder length hair that hadn't seen a comb in years or for that matter any shampoo. But an Alaskan bush pilot is what they were looking for and not some Army Air Corp wussy L-4 Bird Dog fly boy from Ladd Field in Fairbanks. They needed someone that could be motivated with some Army greenbacks. It was a match made in heaven when Wiley Redden sat down at the table. The Old Man knew the going rate was $50/day wet for a small bush plane and pilot. So before Wiley could start with the usual horse-trading, the Old Man spoke,

"Wiley, I had a man attacked, killed and eaten by a pack of six wolves last night. I know you get $ 50/ day, but I am willing to pay you $300/day if you and a sharpshooter can bring me the hides of this wolf pack back to the 95th's camp. I can show you on the map where the attack occurred and the direction of the tracks. You have three days to hunt down, kill and skin the six killer wolves. I have a Regiment of Colored soldiers that have been busting their asses getting this road built to connect Alaska with outside, but not another mile will be cleared until this pack is dead. Do the job in three days, and you get a cool $1000.00. Is that gasoline tank yours?"

"Yes, it is."

"Well, kill those wolves inside of three days and you still get a thousand bucks, and my fuel truck will top your tank off to boot. I have the cash. I will advance you $300 with the balance paid when we see the hides. Do we have a deal?"

It went against Wiley's nature not to try to squeeze another buck or two out of the Army but the Ole Man had offered him more money than he had seen in three months. That $1000 was half what his plane had cost, and he was getting 200 gallons of fuel to boot.

"Yes Sir, we have a deal."

The four sat around the table and plotted the likely escape route of the pack. Wiley said there wasn't but one pack in that area, and the natives had lost a couple of children and sled dogs to them. He said the tribes would be very helpful if it meant killing off this pack. The natives needed the same meat for the winter that the wolves did so they looked at them as competition. Wiley told them he had one of the best shots in Alaska he could use and would be ready to start early tomorrow. They all shook hands and went to bed for the night. The next morning after a hardy breakfast of moose sausage, sawmill gravy and cathead biscuits with molasses syrup topped off with four over-easy eggs, they were ready to see the plane. The yellow and black airplane was a 1939 J-3 Piper Cub with big tundra tires. The big tires were needed to give the prop more clearance so the prop wash wouldn't pick up rocks and propel them into the blades. The big fat tundra tires were the only way to land on unimproved landing strips. Landing on unimproved airstrips was the norm everywhere in Alaska except for Anchorage and Fairbanks. Wiley knew this area of Alaska. The Old Man wanted these wolves found and killed before the HQ even knew about the death. Given ample time, the HQ staff punks could come with another ineffective worthless plan. He figured the runner wouldn't get to HQ before tomorrow afternoon; the staff would have to verify the report and write some briefing paper before the Chief of Staff could be read into the situation. Then the Chief of Staff would inform the General when he returned the following day. So if everything went according to plan, the wolf pack would be dead before they could get any word back to Regiment HQ. The Old Man had told his staff if they received anything back from HQ for" his eyes only," just put it on his desk. One axiom of any large top heavy organization like the Army was you could use the system to your advantage. Don't fight the system, use it!

The pilot and Russ, the sharpshooter, were already at the plane loading up their gear. The wind sock stood straight out as the Alaskan wind roared down the landing strip. The Ole Man handed Wiley his front money and told him they would clear off a small strip for him to land for food and fuel. The two would be put up with the Officers and give any help they needed. All they had to do was to fly and shoot. They would be assigned a transport and driver to go the tribal villages for information on the wolf pack.

Wiley said goodbye and taxied out to the landing strip, pointed his Piper J-3 Cub into the 25 mph easterly headwind and gunned it. The little yellow plane bounced down the strip starting slowly and then accelerating to what appeared to about 35 mph when it jumped off the ground and started to climb due east toward Colored Camp. By the time the Ole Man and the CO climbed into the cab of the transport, the Yellow Cub was out of sight in the emerging morning sun.

The trip back to the company area was quick and uneventful. The temperature had dipped to 20 degrees, and the road was somewhat frozen making the drive bumpy but fast. They made the trip in record time. Upon arrival, Captain Taylor summoned Aaron was by now acting platoon sergeant.

"Sergeant Park, assemble the men in the mess hall tent. I have some information for them. Just so you know before the rest, the Ole Man has authorized and procured an airplane pilot and sharpshooter to hunt down and kill the wolf pack that killed Willie. We will get those sons of bitches and kill every last one. I'll see you in the tent in 15 minutes."

Aaron had gathered up the platoon as the CO has ordered. The CO flanked by the Regimental Commander came into the room as the entire company came to the position of attention as Sgt. Park bellowed "A-TIN-HUT."

"At ease, men. I will get straight to the point. All we can do for Pvt. Willie Wilson is to pray for his soul and his family, and remember him as the good friend and the fine soldier he was. As for the wolves that took his life, we have more options. The Regimental Commander has hired a plane, pilot, and sharpshooter to locate, kill and skin the entire pack. He has three days to complete this mission. The plane will be based here so as soon as we break up, we need to grade a section of this road smooth and long enough for a small plane to land. I'm not a pilot, but I believe a thousand feet runway will suffice. We need to put up a tee shirt, head rag or something on a pole near the runway so the wind can blow it. The flag will tell the pilot what direction to land. We are lucky the prevailing winds are Southeasterly so the road lines up great. I have full faith in this crew to get this airstrip built by evening chow. We may need to line up our trucks with the headlights on if the pilot and shooter are late, and the sun has already set. This pack has killed small children in the native village down the road as well as dog teams. Vengeance will be ours for the vicious attack on our friend. Let get out there and build us a runway. Let do it for Willie!"

The attitude of the men in the tent changed from sadness and frightened to "let's kick some wolf's ass for Willie." The whole platoon couldn't get the airstrip finished soon enough. It was almost like they were on the actual mission to kill the wolf pack. If building this little airstrip could help avenge Willie's death then an airstrip would be built. Aaron was directing the project as a conductor would conduct an orchestra, and the men were responding. All the bulldozers were pushing the pioneer road into a smooth landing surface. Men who were not operating the heavy equipment were using picks and shovels digging up stumps and big rocks ahead of the bulldozers. The J-3 Piper Cub needed less than 1000 feet to land safely and take off in most in any wind condition. Another pair of soldiers was busy cutting down and stripping the limbs off of a spruce tree, so they put the windsock on top. Already some of the trucks had been lined up to illuminate the strip. The pilot and sharpshooter had no idea how much support they had back at 95th's camp. Revenge has a funny way of putting some zip in your step. I doubt if the meanest pack of wolves in the territory could have survived if these men had gotten their hands on them. The harder they worked, the madder and more determined they became. Within a couple of hours, the airstrip was smooth enough even one of the L-4 HQ straphangers pilots could have landed. Once the finishing touches had been completed, everyone broke for chow. That night even K-Rats tasted better than ever before. The Camel cigarettes were as good a four- bit cigar from one of those fancy stores in Chicago. Even the John Wayne chocolate bars were a delight. Just a day before, the entire platoon was so depressed by Willie's horrible mauling death, that the CO didn't have any way to pull them out of their low mental state. Life hadn't been great for the 95th. They had all be drafted from the Deep South and sent to Alaska. They had lost two other men recently, and the Japs were on Alaskan soil. The work was back-breaking hard labor and thankless. Some day they would look back with pride on their mission but that day was way into the future.

As the men enjoyed their K-Rats and Camel cigarettes, the sun was beginning to set. It wasn't dark yet but the temperature was dropping and the night was coming fast. Aaron rallied his men.

"Okay, the lazy bunch of road builders, let's get out there and light up this airstrip. We will all listen for the plane's engine and as soon as anyone hears it blow your whistle and wave. When you men in the trucks hear the signal, turn on your headlights."

After a few minutes, Aaron heard the low roar of a plane. It was hard to judge the distance, but he gave the order to turn on all lights. Within a short time, they saw the outline of a yellow and black high wing airplane that must have been the J-3 Cub. Sure enough, the plane made a circle around the new strip and came down for a landing. The J-3 landed and taxied up the company area. As they got out, every man came up to them and thanked the two for what they were doing. The two sourdoughs were amazed. They had been listening to the white engineers talk about what screw-up lazy bastards' the Colored regiments were. The ole bush pilot knew the white rednecks had lied. He knew the platoon had to have built this airstrip built in a half day or less, and it was better than Ladd Field on most days.

The Captain arrived and led the two into the officer's tent where they had heated up cans of K-Rats for them. The warm can of meat may seem like a small gesture, but warm meat in gravy sure beats cold mystery meat with greasy white lard over it. Add yourself a little Louisiana hot sauce, and you have a first-class meal. The CO had managed to find some 90 proof liquid libations for them to wash down the K-Rats. The two wolfed down the meal in record time having missed lunch. Wiley spoke up and said to the CO,

"Captain, we spotted the trail of the pack, not 10 miles from here. We managed to land at the native village and spoke to the elders about our hunt. They asked if we killed the pack, could they have two hides for their wall for the same reason you do. I told them I couldn't say yes without talking to you first."

"Tell them we will do that for them. We all know how they feel. I will dispatch a report to the Ole Man in the morning to update him on your progress. We have helpers assigned to you as well as transport and driver. We have ample fuel and oil to service your plane. I have assigned a patrol to guard your plane tonight to keep bears from tearing up the fabric. The little black bears haven't bitten anyone yet, but they have ripped up a tarp or two."

The pilot and sharpshooter Russ finished their whiskey and turned in for the night. The CO had ordered big fires built around the perimeter of the company area. The men had been divided into three equal groups for fire and guard duty. This time, all the platoon leaders were armed with M-1 service rifles. The 30-06 round was plenty big enough to kill a wolf or a black bear. Snow had begun to fall so the night visibility was crappy. One thing, however, no one needed to worry about tonight was anybody falling asleep on guard duty. With armed guards carrying 40 rounds each and a third of the company awake at all times, the off-duty men finally, after two sleepless nights, began to fall asleep.

As the morning broke an inch, maybe two, of fresh snow covered the company area. A patrol team was sent out to scan the perimeter for wolf tracks. The CO and Wiley were just finishing a cup of coffee when Sergeant Park reported.

"Sir, you and the pilot should take a look at what we found. The men were out the tent and headed toward the perimeter at a fast pace. The patrol was standing in the area where Willie had been killed. Judging by the tracks in the fresh snow, the pack had returned to eat the remains of their last kill. There was no way to tell how long ago it had been since the pack had left, but Wiley told the CO this was a good sign. The pack's return last night meant they hadn't killed anymore and would be on the prowl hunting for food. The contrast of dark wolves against the fresh snow gave them the best chance to find the pack. The plane had been serviced, and the wings cleared off. The mess hall crew had made them a lunch that, of course, was K-Rats of their choice with some cheese and white bread sandwiches just for good measures. Somewhere the mess tent Sarge found a quart jar filled with hot coffee and wrapped the jar in brown paper to keep it warm. If anyone in an Army unit could find something, it's the mess Sergeant, the motor pool Sergeant or the supply Sergeant. The little yellow Cub fired right up, taxied to the strip and roared down the dirt runway throwing snow so high and thick one wondered if they could see at all. But as soon as the men were starting to get concerned, the yellow plane popped out above the snow and flew away in the direction of the tracks.

The CO had asked the platoon leaders if they thought the men were ready to start construction again. They all agreed while the plane was out looking for the pack; they would welcome the work. All the bulldozer operators and the pick and ax crews set out to build another mile or two of the highway. The work was a little easier in cold weather since the ground was freezing up at night. Sometime in the last few weeks the mosquitoes and flies had slowly gone away to wherever they go to in the winter. The crew figured they would die over the winter if it got cold enough. Oh, if only that were true.

Along about 1400 hours, as they were taking a break, shots were heard in the distance. They tried to count but some said it was six, some said eight and one swore he counted eleven. The buddies kidded him telling since he didn't take his boots off; he couldn't count over ten.

CHAPTER 11

THE KILL SHOT

Wiley was flying at an altitude of 150-200 feet above the ground to
see the wolves' tracks better. Russ, the shooter was looking out the
side in the distance while Wiley kept his attention on the terrain and
the tracks. Russ had with him his two favorite weapons, a Winchester
Model 94 30/30 lever action rifle and a Parker side by side 12 gauge
shotgun. The Parker, loaded with Double "ought" (or 00) buckshot,
the ammo he had selected for maximum injury to the wolves. If only
one shot of the nine 30 caliber size pellets struck the target, the wolf
would not be able to run far away and would suffer a slow painful
death. The wolf would, depending on the location of the pellet,
bleed out in just a few minutes and would most likely be howling in
pain. The loud mournful noise made by the dying wolf would make
the savage canine much easier to find and skin. The skinning was
necessary since a pelt proved a kill and required for payment. All
Alaskans believed in the practice of conservation. No bullet would
be wasted to put the wolf out of its misery if they found the animal
still alive but dying. Willie got no bullet. Yes sir, a little Wild West
style skinning alive would the order of the day. The wolf would be
fully aware of his situation as the skinner's knife cut through the belly

fur, ripped up to and around the neck. You see, a wolf can live for a short time without its fur, but the removal would inflict pain beyond any pain the wolf had ever known. That's just a little irony of life for a creature that on almost a daily basis inflicted the same pain on a newborn moose calf or a small village child without any hesitation. Now, for a very short period, this killing machine would feel that same pain before dying. It's not as much fun when you are not on top of the food chain anymore.

Wiley had picked up a good trail to follow. The pack was heading into a delta that stretched for miles. The plane was being bounced around by some clear air turbulence and a twenty-five mph crosswind. Both worked to Russ's advantage since Wiley had to crab the plane to the left (an aviation term that means to adjust the yaw of a plane to ensure a certain ground path). This crabbing flight maneuver made a shot out the right window much easier. The quartering headwind silenced the prop signature for long enough to allow the plane to get into range for Russ's Winchester. Wiley had hunted from the air many times before. Hunting, for Alaskans, was not for a trophy to mount on their den wall. Nor was it something to brag about to all their whitetail deer hunting buddies in Dallas like the hunters from "outside" were so famous for. Bringing back meat for a long winter was the most important item on the agenda in Alaska in the fall. Wiley had hunted with Russ many times before. They were like a highly trained fighter plane aircrew that knew each other needs and thoughts. Wiley also knew how to maneuver the Cub into position for Russ's shots. The quartering 25 mph headwind would work perfectly with the Cub's slow stall speed of 38 mph. Allowing for the speed of the pace of the pack (around five mph at a trot or as much as 25 mph in a short sprint), Wiley could position the plane for Russ at a relative speed of almost zero. Giving the appearance of hovering above the animals would be the most advantageous shot. Wiley would drop down to 10-15 feet off the ground for the best shot placement. This aircraft maneuver was risky since, in the event of an engine failure, crashing into the terrain was unavoidable. This maneuver was a calculated risk and one worth taking. Russ and Wiley figured they easily could drop three or four of the slowest wolves. Most likely, they would be the females and young pups (women and children first) off in a couple of passes but the alpha male and the older wolves would have to be hunted alone. Wolves adapt quickly to a changing environment. Russ knew that if the wolf pack was spotted several miles into the delta, Wiley could maneuver using the Cub like a border collie herding sheep to keep the pack turned inward. By not allowing them to escape into the woods or brushy areas, they could pick off the remainder as they tired from running. The J-3 Piper Cub was a frugal lady when it came to fuel consumption, sipping only 5 gallons per hour. With a 12 gallon tank and a five-gallon "jerry" can (an easy method of storing fuel on the back rack of an Army Jeep) in the back of the seat; Wiley could hunt wolves for three hours before heading back to his fuel cache. His fuel cache contained four more jerry cans of fuel for four more hours of flying. The limiting factor keeping the Cub in the air for the longest possible time wasn't the fuel consumption but the crew's asses and bladders. As the fuel tank emptied, the crew's bladders filled. As good as cookie's coffee was it had to come out sometime. Wiley had stashed sleeping bags and K-Rats back at the fuel cache just in case of bad weather. He had made an arrangement with the native village elders if he didn't fly over the village by nightfall to get them with their dog teams.

People with different backgrounds and lifestyles can work together when they have a common enemy, like the wolf pack.

Anticipation was high inside the 1939 J-3 Piper Cub as the day's flight entered its second hour. Wiley was doing some mental math figuring out when he was going to have to break off the hunt to refuel. He still had the five-gallon jerry can in the back. But he decided to wait until either they killed something or nature called to land and refuel. Just then, Russ yelled loudly and pointed out to his right,

"The bastards are over at 2 O'clock!"

Wiley, being familiar with the military term for spotting other aircraft immediately looked about 20 degrees to the right of the ground track of the Cub and saw the pack. Judging by the speed of the pack, Wiley concluded the pack was unaware of their presence. What a textbook set up for a kill. Wiley adroitly maneuvered the Cub to a path slightly to the pack's left so the wind could mask the engine noise as long as possible. He planned to approach the pack from behind as he angled the plane across their path where he would give Russ a shot outside the right window. Wiley knew well the small area Russ would be able to fire and avoid hitting the prop, strut or tires. Wiley would soon have to summon all his piloting skills, even the ones that always surfaced after a few beers with other pilots.

The pack was trotting along with the big alpha male in the lead. None of the wolves had even looked back as Wiley set up Russ for his first shot, a young pup trailing the pack by a large margin. Since the pilot of a Cub was in front of the passenger in the back seat, Wiley couldn't sight the rifle from his seat. Wiley had slowed the plane to about 40 mph that with the quartering headwind providing Russ with a sight picture slowing coming into firing position. Just like he would lead a duck or goose, Russ picked his time and fired. The pup dropped down and rolled a few times and never moved again. One wolf was down and five to go. Russ had five rounds left in his Model 94's magazine and already was taking aim at his next victim. The headwind had muffled the engine and gunshot noise enough that the pack wasn't even aware of the death from above on their trail. Russ's next target was a small female that did manage to look up at the last second before the crack of the 30/30 round rang out, the last sound she would ever hear. Now the score was wolves one, 95th Engineers two. This time, the noise got all of the pack's attention because that leisurely pace of 5 mph picked up to around 20 mph. This new pace was still no challenge for the Wiley and Russ wolf killing team. Wiley, being the hunter, picked out the weakest and slowest remaining member of the pack. The target turned out to be a large wolf that seemed to run a little slower than the rest. The pack as expected had split up into lone wolves, scattering in all directions, so Wiley zeroed in on the next soon to be a dead wolf. Although this wolf was slow, he could change directions pretty damn fast. This directional change necessitated that Wiley violently banks the Cub into some very uncomfortable flight configurations to place the aircraft into position for Russ's next shot. Russ had as much faith in Wiley flying skills as Wiley had in Russ's marksmanship. After a minute, Wiley set Russ up for his next shot. The wolf was slowing down as the plane lined up for the kill shot. The wolf turned and looked up at the yellow object in the sky. With his tongue hanging out the side of his foamed up mouth, the old wolf saw the smoke and fire from the 30/30 muzzle, felt something hit his side like a brick that burned like hell. The round immediately felled him. As he rolled on the ground, the wolf could feel the pain intensify. Although not dead yet, he most certainly was dying. He might wish for a quick death but that's wasn't on the agenda for today.

With half the pack killed, Wiley and Russ knew they must contain the pack in the open delta if they were to finish the job today.

Wiley could see all the wolves and calculated it would take them at least 20-30 minutes to make it into the tree line. There was no way that was going to happen if Wiley had anything to say about it. He picked out the wolf the most further distance away and headed for him. The Cub overtook the wolf in short order and Wiley the pilot morphed into Wiley, the flying Border Collie. A low pass in front of a wolf will almost assure a change in direction which it did. All you had to do is let the wolf stay ahead of the plane and let him run. A scared and tired wolf will make mistakes in judgment. After heading one wolf back into the center of the delta, Wiley set his sights on another one close to a small bunch of brush. Although not as much cover as a tree line, sheltering there would require Wiley and Russ to land and disembark to flush them out. The crew had lost sight of the third wolf that appeared to be the biggest of the pack; the alpha male. This big dominate male had domain over the pack. A challenge could be made to the alpha male, but the challenger better be prepared to fight to the finish.

With one wolf missing and one hiding in a bunch of brushes, Wiley and Russ decided to take down the other wolf. They lined up for a shot but as they got close the wolf although exhausted, cut hard to the left, and the plane overshot the target. Wiley banked the plane hard right to re-engage the wolf, but a little buffeting on the controls told Wiley to decrease the angle of attack before he stalled the plane. Wiley took a little bank out and lowered the nose slightly to correct this potentially fatal situation, but this much-needed diversion of attention had caused him to lose the wolf. With their heads looking in all directions for a wolf, no one was paying any attention to the fuel. Soon the fuel would get their undivided attention. They spotted the tired wolf heading back in his original direction. Wiley decided the other wolves could wait so the pursuit was afoot. Wiley knew he had ample time to set the next shot up for Russ so he lagged back so the wolf would slow down. He now was flying with a tailwind, so he was catching the wolf too fast. A headwind would be the ideal shot situation, so he made a wide circle getting the plane in front of the wolf. A low pass and the wolf turned back into the wind as Wiley wanted. Russ already had his rifle out the window as Wiley set him perfectly the speed of the plane and wolf meshed into a textbook shot. The 30/30 round penetrated the backbone dead in the center of the wolf. This killing machine, which had eaten his last moose calf or native baby, fell to the tundra dead. Four wolves were now dead or dying with only two left to go. Skinning would have to wait until the whole pack was put down.

The clump of brush the wolf had decided to hide in was a good landmark for navigation on flat, barren tundra. Wiley pointed the Cub toward the brush as Russ was patting himself on the back for his four for four shot record. Maybe a little less self-congratulation and little more reloading would have been a better use of his time, a fact he would soon find out. As Wiley reached the site and started to bank around the clump of bushes, a sound no pilot likes to hear filled the cockpit. The sound of engine starved for fuel is something you will ever forget. Running out of gas on the way to work is a pain in the ass and embarrassing but in the air its crap city. The little wire sticking up out of the tank was right in front of Wiley, but he had forgotten about the flight time due to the chase. The 1939 J-3 Cub had no fuel gauge inside the cockpit; it had no electrical system to run it had there been one. What it had installed was a very effective float system. A wire connected to a floating piece of cork that bobbed up and down inside the fuel tank. Present company excepted; this was a foolproof method; nothing to break. If you looked at the wire, you could see marks that indicated the remaining fuel. Naturally, both Wiley and Russ immediately looked at the indicator wire only to see no marks and not much wire sticking out of the tank. Yes, they were out of fuel, and the landing strip is whatever was in front of them. Wiley's skill and coolness paid off as he deadsticked the now silent Cub onto the tundra about 100 yards away from the brush pile. The silver lining was, with no engine running and landing into the wind, they had arrived without spooking the wolf in the brush.

With three pressing matters to accomplish; Refueling the plane, killing the other two wolves and peeing (and not necessarily in that order), the two decided to kill the closest wolf first, probably the best choice. They didn't have an eyeball on the hiding wolf but decided to cover opposite sides of the batch of the brush so both would have a shot. Wiley had Russ's Parker side by side shotgun, and both chambers were loaded. Russ had brought plenty of ammo for both guns and had safely stored it behind the rear seat on the plane. Any pilot knows the three most useless things in the world is runway behind you, altitude above you and gas left in the airport fuel tank. For these so far successful hunters, their list of the most useless things will start with the ammo you left at home.

The little batch of brush was small but dense which made seeing the wolf all but impossible. Wiley and Russ knew better than to go into the brush. Instead, they made noise and threw sticks into the brush. Soon out of the tangle of weeds and scrub brush bolted a tired wolf that appeared to be still trying to catch his breath. The canine bolted out in the direction of Russ, who managed to fire two shots that completely missed. Wiley having heard all the commotion and shooting came running as fast as he could run. Wiley moved pretty damn fast for a man of forty-three who had eaten three fried eggs, moose sausage and cathead biscuits with blackstrap molasses every day since before he started wearing long pants, As his friend and the wolf came into sight, Wiley immediately perceived the danger. The wolf was circling Russ, who as good a shot as he was, had discovered some gaps in his math education. He had emptied his Winchester 94, and now all he had was a very pissed off wolf and a rifle that now was nothing more than a metal bat to defend him. Russ looked over not 75 yards from where he now stood and saw the Cub, which housed 100 rounds of 30/30 ammo and 100 12 gauge 00 buckshot shells.

> *"Damn, the ammo might as well be back in Fairbanks at the hardware store for all the good it's doing me now. Now that's something they don't teach you in school but should."*

The wolf had Russ lined up in his sights and was ready for the kill. The wolf looked around to see what was making the racket that, of course, was Wiley. Wiley raised the shotgun being very careful not to hit Russ. Before Wiley could squeeze off a round, the wolf jumped and landed on Russ. The sharp teeth of the wolf were tearing through the clothing and starting to tear at the flesh. Wiley was on top of the wolf, hitting and stabbing it with his ever-present skinning knife. Wiley had thrown the shotgun down because he was afraid if he shot he would hit Russ. The wolf turned to Wiley and jumped on him, who started doing a good job of stabbing the animal. Russ hadn't been hurt badly but couldn't use his right hand due to the defensive wounds from fending off the attack. He managed to pull his other hunting knife out with his left hand and went to Wiley's defense. Being a one-handed knife fighter wasn't the easiest thing he had ever done, but he managed to deliver several lethal blows to the wolf's neck and belly. The blows slowed down but did not stop the wolf's assault. Wiley still had the use of both hands since most of his wounds were on his arms. Russ had managed one-handedly to throw the wolf to the ground and away from Wiley. Wiley pounded on the dying wolf, stabbing it so many times; he lost count. The wolf hadn't moved in a minute, but Wiley continued his killing frenzy. Russ finally had to pull him off of the carcass.

As they sat in the blood covered snow, the adrenaline rush they had only seconds before started to subside. A minute before Wiley or Russ could have moved heaven and earth, but now all they had was a headache, shaking hands, a desire to throw up and a backache. They assessed their respective injuries and used some handkerchiefs to wipe off the blood. They both knew these wounds weren't life threatening but had to be tended to before the infection set in. As pretty as the Alaskan and Yukon scenery is, deadly infections lurk on the ground, in the water and most certainly in the mouths of wolves.

"Well Russ ole buddy, this story ought to be worth a free beer or two back at the bar."

"You can bet your ass on that one. You were a wild man with that knife. Just look at the blood all over you. Most of it must be the wolf's since you don't look again worst for the wear."

Of the three things they had to do, the only thing that remained was the refueling of the plane. First, they had killed the wolf and second; that potty break was no longer needed since both had lost all bladder control during the wolf attack. Russ was still trying to catch his breath, and Wiley was about to rise and go to the plane when out of the blue, Wiley was knocked over by an unseen overwhelming force. The alpha male had been found or more correctly, he had found them. Nobody knows if wolves think like humans but if they do, one can only imagine what was going through his mind as he faces the killers of his pack. Only minutes after Wiley and Russ had a near death encounter with one of the wolf pack, the sole remaining member, and leader of the pack was out for revenge. This male was bigger and more ferocious than any of the other pack members. He seemed to have a battle plan that had included waiting until the two humans had worn them self out before attacking. Where had that tactic been used today?

Hindsight is always 20/20. Just after the attack was over, and the fifth wolf was dead, sitting on their asses seemed to be just the right thing to do for Wiley and Russ. Now a few of those 30/30 rounds and a pocket full of shotgun shells would be a nice addition to this new situation. Two wolf attacks on the same day are just bad luck or bad Karma. Russ had at least gotten the use of both hands back after the adrenaline rush had vanished.

The big male was standing on Wiley's back looking at Russ. The 12 gauge shotgun was on the ground between Russ and the wolf. No one knows if the wolf knew if that piece of wood and steel posed any threat to him or not. Russ knew however if he and his friend were to survive this new attack; the shotgun had to be retrieved. Wiley hadn't been hurt unless you count having the breath knocked out of you by a 150-pound gray wolf. Wiley could see the standoff between Russ and the wolf, but he was helpless due to the weight of this monster wolf on his back. He remembered his ever-present little nickel plated 38 snub-nosed revolver he had in his side pocket. He had been packing this ole friend for so long; he had forgotten he had it on his person. Wiley figured a caveman didn't leave his cave without his club, so he was never far from his Smith and Wesson. Most of the time, he, when he had to use his 38, was when wild Alaskan animals misbehaved. Not that a 38 was any defense against a bear that had its sights set on you for supper, but it just might be enough for a chance encounter between a Mama bear and her cubs. At any rate, the S&W wheel gun was the only game in town. Wiley tried to reach his pocket that contained the revolver but was afraid he would prompt the wolf into an attack.

The standoff between Russ and the wolf seemed to last for an hour but in reality only lasted a few seconds. Russ summoned all the strength and courage contained within him and jumped toward the shotgun. At almost the same instance, the wolf leaped toward him. Russ reached the shotgun before the big male could attack him. As he grabbed the stock of the vintage Parker, the wolf clamped down on his right arm with such force Russ involuntarily dropped the gun and gripped the nape of the neck of the giant wolf. Wiley had managed to retrieve his Smith and Wesson 38 caliber revolver. As he tried to aim at the wolf, some part of Russ's body seemed to keep getting into the line of fire. The alpha male almost outweighed Russ and in his weaken state he couldn't last very long against this killing machine. Wiley knew he had to take a chance on a shot. He took aim at the part of the wolf that posed the least threat to Russ. He fired, and the bullet hit the big wolf in the belly. The bullet traveled through the wolf's vital organs and managed to nick most every one of them. The shot would cause internal bleeding but not instant death. They still had a big badass wolf to kill. Unfortunately for Russ, Wiley's 38 caliber bullet went into his leg. The pain and the burning almost caused him to pass out, but he knew that would fatal. He instead drew his hunting knife and began stabbing the monster anywhere he could. Wiley lined up another shot and fired. This shot hit the beast in the hind quarters causing him to spin around in a circle. This momentary lapse was the break Russ had needed to pick up his Parker shotgun and fire at point blank range at the wolf. Both barrels of the 12 gauge fire almost the same time. Eighteen pellets from the two 00 buckshot shells blasted their way into the side of the wolf. Death was instantaneous as the pellets blew the wolf's heart into a million pieces and onto the snow-covered tundra.

Ding Dong, the wolf is dead!

Just in case there were more wolves. Wiley and Russ made a beeline to the Cub and reloaded both weapons. Russ crammed about ten extra rounds into his side pocket. In the future when he and his Winchester left the cabin, he would always carry at least ten extra rounds with him. This close call with death had made a believer out of him. You may be on the top of the food chain with a loaded gun but without ammo, you are just more difficult to kill.

Wiley always had a small first aid kit with him, so he field dressed Russ's leg wound. Thank God the bullet missed the femoral artery, or Russ would have bled out during the fight. However, as they say in the western picture shows, it was only a flesh wound. The two started skinning out the wolves, and the work went fast since they weren't concerned with preserving the meat.

With the plane refueled and the pelts behind the back seat, the two were off to the 95th International Airstrip, which was a correct term since the strip was in Canada and the plane landing was from Alaska. They made a pass over the company area and turned on final for a landing. The 95th had improved another 1500 feet of the airstrip. This runway length was now over 2500 feet and long enough for C-47 Gooney Bird, the plane the Army Air Corp used for troop and cargo transport, to land. Ladd Field in Fairbanks should be so lucky to have a runway this smooth and flat with no trees at the approach or departure ends of the runway. Wiley taxied the Cub over to his tiedown spot and unloaded the pelts of the killer pack. They segregated the big alpha male as if anyone couldn't pick it out. This freak of nature was 30% larger than the biggest wolf anybody had ever seen in these parts of the woods. That's saying a lot since wolf packs have been roaming the tundra as long as anyone can remember.

In a few minutes, every man made his way to see the pelts. Captain Taylor dispatched a driver to alert the Ole Man the mission had been a success The CO also put a little reminder in the note to please bring their money, sir.

All the men were happier than they had ever been since leaving their hometowns. Some danced on the pelt while some spit on them. After a little more celebration, Aaron told them to return to work. Willie's slaughter had been avenged, and things were back to normal in Colored Camp.

The medic had been called in to administer more intense first aid. He gave them tetanus shots and dressed the wounds after cleaning them. He told the CO they should be treated soon before infection sets in. The mess sergeant delivered some soup and cold sandwiches to Wiley and Russ. They were starved, after all, the excitement earlier in the day, so they thanked the Sarge and wolfed down (pun intended) their well-deserved meal. After lunch, Wiley and Russ told the CO the drama that had transpired earlier that morning. The CO just sat stunned as they told how they became the hunted and almost lost their lives in the battle. Wiley suggested he deliver the two pelts to the village now so he could depart for home as soon as he got paid. The CO told him to go. The village needed closure just like his men, and he was glad to accommodate the village. Wiley and Russ departed for the village that by air wasn't but a 10-minute flight. The CO drafted a letter for the Ole Man instructing the HQ Camp Hospital to treat these men's injuries because they were sustained in the line of duty. He also wrote a recommendation for outstanding service to the war effort for the elimination of the threat to the 95th Colored Engineer Regiment.

In an hour, Wiley and Russ returned from the village just as the Ole Man arrived. The CO briefed him on the wolf pack kill. The Ole Man signed both letters the CO had drafted, paid the men and thanked them for their great work. Wiley and Russ taxied out to the new 2500 foot airstrip, rolled down the strip and flew off to the west heading for Alaska.

Aaron suggested that the pelts be cut into smaller pieces for the men as reminders what fate awaits those who mess with the US Army. Death will be swift, certain and in-kind. Aaron would carry his strip of fur with him through the entire war.

CHAPTER 12

WINTER ARRIVES IN THE YUKON

The road construction was ahead of schedule, so the 95th was pulled from road construction in the Yukon and moved south to British Columbia for the Sikanna Chief River Bridge project. A bridge had to be built over this river before the winter freeze and that time was fast approaching. The termination dust was down to the valley floor, and all the signs were the never ending snow was to begin. The civil engineers estimate for this project was five weeks with a trained crew. HQ in Fairbanks figured the 95th would screw it up so badly the white boys would be called in to salvage the project. Since the Japs had been contained on the Aleutian Islands after their short offensive, the grandson of a Confederate War General could revive his racist attack on the Colored engineer regiments. The Aleutian Islands campaign would be costly, but the possibility of the Japs advancing any closer to mainland Alaska was diminishing. The Japs had attacked Midway and gotten their asses handed to them by the US Navy. First, Jimmy Doolittle bombed their precious capital of Tokyo, and now Admiral Nimitz's Pacific Fleet had sent them limping back to Japan with their Imperial tails tucked under their asses. They couldn't drink enough rice wine to forget that ass whooping. The

Japs, since their attack on Pearl Harbor, had lost almost all their aircraft carriers and planes as well as their most experienced aircrews. These losses were too great ever to recover. The sleeping giant had indeed been awakened as Admiral Yamamoto had feared and was pissed off.

When the unit arrived at the Sikanna Chief River, a small camp had been set up for what most figured to be a long winter project. The five horsepower sawmill was already cutting bridge timbers for the project, and the Southern end of the road was in sight. Tents had been set up for the men, so Aaron guided them over them to stow their gear. The CO was meeting with the civil engineer in charge when Aaron reported.

"Sgt. Park, I would like to introduce you to Mr. Swenson, our engineer. He will be in charge of the bridge construction. Consider anything he says to the same as if I had said it, understand?'

Captain Taylor knew Aaron understood the engineer was in charge, but the instructions were for Mr. Swenson's ear.

"Yes Sir, Captain. I understand. I am pleased to meet you, Sir."

"I have told Mr. Swenson you're the best supervisor I have ever had. Do the 95th proud."

Mr. Swenson, the CO, and Aaron sat down at the field table and began to develop a plan of action. Mr. Swanson said," The most pressing and critical phase of the bridge construction will the setting of the pilings that supports the bridge. This phase has to be done first and before the hard freeze comes. The weather forecast isn't on our side. An Arctic cold front is building and forecasted to move into the area in three or four days. If that cold front arrives and the pilings aren't in by then, the whole project will be on hold until spring. If the weather delays the bridge completion, then your unit will have to winter over here. It appears the road building phase is scheduled to be finished by early next month. Washington has put a top priority on the completion this year. I have been here supervising the stockpiling of all the materials needed to complete this work. I will need some help from your men that has sawmill experience to boost the timber production. The men running the mill want to get out of here as bad as everyone else. I believe we can do this on time, but the weather front worries the hell out of me. What do you think, Sgt. Park?"

"Sir, once I tell the men if this bridge is built in 2 weeks, we can leave this cold ass place, there will be no stopping them. I have several good sawmill hands that worked the pine tree country of South Mississippi. They have been great in the past on all things wood, Sir."

"Aaron, May I call you Aaron?"

No one before the Army had ever given a damn about whether I liked what they had called me. And all of them were white folks. How come they didn't live in Mississippi?"

"No sir, I mean Yes sir, I don't mind. It might take a while to get a little time used to, though."

Mr. Swenson continued, "All right. By the way, you don't have to Sir me and Mr. Swenson was my father. You call me Ervin."

Ervin laid out an ambitious plan to get the pilings installed in two days. First water had to be diverted around the area where the pilings were to be built. A wall of timbers needed to be stacked up and secured so the water could be pumped out. Next pilings would be driven into the river bed with this floating platform barge with a pile driver mounted on it. Finally, mesh wire sort of like hog wire would line the timbers and river rock would be used to fill it to the top. Mr. Swenson had designed a two river piling bridge instead of a three pilings. The civil engineers in the War Department would be too busy to check up until after it was built, and traffic was moving to Alaska. Then they would probably take credit for the change. This change would give the 95th a slim chance of completing the bridge pilings phase before the storm front arrived. The superstructure could be constructed in bad weather but not the cold, wet portion. Some poor ole Southern Colored boys would have to freeze their asses off to get the pilings done.

"Well Aaron, if you have no questions, the time to start is now. The work will be around the clock until at least the piling work is done. I need you to pick out those sawmill hands and sent to the plant. You might go with them to introduce them to the crew. They will glad to see your men. Then have the rest report to the river's edge next to the pile driving barge. I will brief them on the plan. Think you can do all that in 30 minutes?"

"Yes, Sir, I mean Erwin."

Aaron raced over to the tent. For the first time since getting to Alaska and Canada, he had heard about the end of the project. He couldn't wait to tell the men. As bad as the old camp was in the last few months it had become home. Now they had packed up and moved to the side of a river. The north sky looked dark and gray with snow slowing dropping out of the sky. They had arrived in Alaska what normal people who call winter but was springtime in Alaska. It had been twenty degrees for long periods early on, and nobody was looking forward to a full blown Alaskan winter.

"Men, listen up. I have been briefed on the project, and I have some great news. This whole damn highway project is almost complete. As a matter of fact, the work you can see to the east is the last section. Crews from the other direction and that crew will meet in a few weeks. That's the good news. Now brace yourself for the bad news. We have to finish this bridge in 2 weeks, or we will have to winter over. The pilings are the hardest part, which are the parts that go into the water that holds up the bridge. A smart and very nice man named Mr. Swenson has got us a plan to get it done. You see there's a bad bunch of weather headed this way that will freeze everything up. If those pilings are in, we can finish the damn thing and leave this cold ass place. Where ever we get reassigned to is better than here. Men, it's up to us to get them pilings in before that storm hits. We gots us two maybe three days before the big freeze hits. Some of you will be getting wet. They got some rubber pants, but it will be cold and dangerous. Also all you South Mississippi and Louisiana boys that got sawmill experience will be working in the mill. The timber needs to be sawn while we are putting in the pilings. We have always worked as a team but now is the time for our best effort. The CO believes we can do this and so do I. Let's show these white folks what Colored men from the South can do. Now, you sawmill hands follow me. When I return, the rest of us will be going to the river. Let's get out of this cold dark place."

Aaron walked the sawmill hands over to the mill site. After the short introductions, the men started to work. They were used to this type of small generator driven mills. The big mills didn't hire Colored folks, but the small mills did and didn't pay as well as the Army.

Aaron returned to fetch the rest of the unit. A good leader can sense the morale of his unit. There was an energy among those members of the 95th Colored Engineer Regiment and that energy was about to be released on the bridge over the Sikanna Chief River. Aaron told the men what an honor it would be to have finished the final phase of this historic highway in record time. Not that anyone outside would ever hear, but the unit would know and be proud.

Sergeant Park marched his men over to the river where Ervin was standing. He wanted the main man first impression of the unit to be stellar.

"Unit, halt. Right face. Stand at ease."

"Sir, Company C of the 95th Colored Engineer Regiment is reporting for duty."

"Thank you, Aaron," the engineer said. "This looks a fine bunch of men that's ready to build a bridge. Stand at ease to me means just come over here and sit down where you all can hear and see me. As I have told Aaron, I am a civilian, and you don't have to call me sir."

As the men moved closer to the river, they were sizing up the new guy. Erwin Swenson stood 6'5" with not an ounce of fat on him. What they didn't know was that Swenson had been an All-America football player in college where he earned his degree in civil engineering in December 1941, two weeks after the Jap attack on Pearl Harbor. He had volunteered for Officer Candidate School (OCS or 90-day wonders as some NCOs had dubbed them) only to fail his physical due to a previously undiagnosed heart mummer. The next day his father called his senator who chaired the Armed Service

Committee in the US Senate to see if the Army Corp of Engineers could find a place for his son.

Sometimes luck comes as a result of timing because unknown to the general public; the Alaskan-Canadian Highway was about as high a priority as any project in the War Department. An All-America football player from the Senator's Alma Mater was about to be given one of the most prized projects in the war.

Ervin began addressing the men,

"Gentlemen, we have the final phase of this highway project here at the Sikanna Chief River Bridge. Time is not on our side. The weather forecast gives us maybe two or three days before a hard freeze hits the area. Once the river freezes, the piling work has to stop. If we can get the pilings in place, then neither hell nor high water will keep us from finishing the bridge and leaving this God forsaken place once and for all. I don't know about you men, but I have seen enough mosquitoes, moose, wolves, ass deep mud and spruce trees to last me a lifetime.

What you men say we get out here and build us a bridge."

Man, this engineer sure knows how to fire up troops. Too bad Erwin wasn't an officer, Aaron thought to himself. From what he had seen of Officers of the 95th except for the CO and the Ole Man, Mr. Swenson was head and shoulders above them.

Colored Camp was fired up. The troops were throwing their hats high in the air and shouting. The job of building and setting the piling was the coldest and most dangerous. But they had more than enough volunteers. One of the men working in the mill came over to Aaron and said,

"The boss man down to the mill sent me up here to fetch more help to move the bigger timbers closer to the river. We need a few hands for a couple of hours."

Aaron told him to pick anyone not on the list to go into the water.

This piling operation was harder than it looked. The first four poles to go in the river were the biggest, heaviest and tallest of the bridge parts. The river at this time of year was shallow, but the pilings had to be engineered to withstand spring floods and all the trees and logs that the snow melt flushed down the river. The survey crew had placed markers all over the place. Out in the river were four big red halibut buoys just bobbing up and down as the river raced by. These buoys marked the spot where the center poles had to be set. The rock encasements had to be large enough to hold two poles set eighteen feet apart. The construction company had leased two of the biggest and most powerful backhoes Caterpillar had to offer. These backhoes could dig the holes down for several feet and backfill after the poles were set. No other time of the year could even these giant machines perform the task of the placement of the eight 35 foot 24"x 18" treated timbers. These timbers would be paired and coupled together to form four large pilings. These four massive timbers had to be raised and shored up at the precise intervals drawn on the plans, or most of the other precut timbers would not fit. Surveyors and their transits were supposed to make sure the timbers were lined up plumb and true. Managing engineering construction projects in the field with little or no resources wasn't taught in school. It seemed ole Ervin had a little Yankee resourcefulness in his blood. The crew had a floating pile driver, big ass backhoes, even bigger bulldozers and more pumps than you could count at their disposal. The CO asked Ervin how he was able to swing all this equipment when the 95th had been given the short end of the stick this whole project. Ervin confided in him the following story.

It seemed the General Jefferson's racist tactics had been noticed by too many people who had contacts far above his pay grade. When the Top Brass at the War Department got a few calls from Congress conveying their collective unhappiness about the conduct of General Jefferson, they decided to give this bridge project all the support it could while bypassing Alaska Command. The best news was that the General's first clue he had been outflanked by Washington would be a call from his boss congratulating him on the early completion of the Alaskan-Canadian Highway.

"He will have no choice but to give your men a unit citation." Erwin said.

The first order of business was to set the dams to divert the flow of water around the spot where the pilings are to be driven. The mill had already constructed and treated the dam walls that needed to be lowered into the river. A V-shaped wooden dam would be manuvered into the river on the upstream side of the piling areas marked by the big halibut buoys. Then the floating platform would be moved to the downstream side and will set the two other dams in place. This enclosure would form a corral around the site where the engineers have marked for the insertion spots of the pilings. The next hour would be the most dangerous and critical phase of the bridge construction project. Even if the dams go in smoothly, men will have to be dropped into the center of these unanchored dams in cold water before the pumps can begin to drain the site. The dams were construced out of wood that floats, there is a chance the current will, after a short period, move these dams enough to allow swift-flowing water and debris to flood the chambers. This situation would almost assuredly cause the men inside to be swept downstream to their deaths. Textbooks and slide rules can't calculate or negate this sort of danger.

Sometimes the enemy that could kill you doesn't wear a uniform.

Under the watchful eye of the CO, Ervin, and Sgt Park, the critical phase began. The big crane gingerly lifted the first dam up off the platform's deck and started to maneuver the big wooden contraption into place. The mill crew had made sure the walls were high enough so the water would not flow over the top. A river depth varies with drainage upstream, and the information is very spotty at best, so these mill-hands added a little height for good measure. The first dam settled into the river without incidence as shouts and cheers rang out from the onlookers on the river bank. One section was down, and three left to go. The second dam caught a puff of the wind as the crane operator was swinging it around from the deck. The engineers feared the dams didn't have the strength alone without the adjoining downstream section to withstand the stress. The crew was silent as the large wooden structure osculated in the wind. All the crane operator could do was to stop and hope the wind died down, and the dam would settle down. Everybody's attention was focused on the platform and its cargo, realizing that so much was at stake. Forget the fact a cold winter in the Great North for the 95th was riding on the crane operator's skill; the highway couldn't open until this bridge was in operation. A year ago most of the men of the 95th could have cared less about the country that had suppressed their people for hundreds of years. But now after seeing the whole nation wasn't like the South, they had grown, and a new sense of pride and honor had been instilled in them. Yes, sir, these men were now a part of the US Army. Being in a separate unit would be fine, for now.

Many silent prayers were being sent to the Lord, and their prayers were answered. The wind calmed down as fast as it had started, and the wooden dam settled down. The crane operator wasted no time in maneuvering the dam into place as everyone breathed a sigh of relief. As the preacher always said, Thank you, Lord, Thank you.

With the upstream dams in place, it was time to set the other two that would mate up and make the water columns that needed to be drained. The river crew was on the platform along with Aaron, who had moved on deck from the river bank. He wasn't going to be too far away from his men on this dangerous stage of construction. The pilot slowly moved the big platform around the dams and into position for the final operation. Everyone's nerves were on end as the pilot set the anchor and the engine power to hold the barge for the third dam section. If this positioning goes without a hitch, the 95th would be walking in tall cotton as the Southern saying goes. The crane operator began the lift with the precision of airline pilot coming into a cloud covered runway on an instrument approach. Not a rough movement or a jerk on the controls as he picked the first of two remaining dam sections. Now as before, everyone was silent as they said a few prayers. Having learned from the errant dam caught by the wind, the crew had attached tether lines from each side to control the osculation effect of the wind. The operation went flawlessly as the dam settled into the perfect place. The engineers had the mill crew drill two-inch holes into the sides vertically so spikes could be driven into the riverbed to anchor the structure down. They knew once the water was out, the current could pick up the whole unit and sent it downstream with everyone inside. Metal straps with predrilled holes for smaller spikes would be pounded in the top timbers of the dams to connect the two halves. All of this work must be accomplhished by the men in the cold glacier fed river water before pumping could begin.

Like a well-trained crew that had been working on projects like this for years, the men of the 95th jumped into the water and began their work. The platform had rigged up a smaller driver for the spikes so they could be driven into the riverbed. The straps were being installed by a pair of ten-pound hammers. The crew had on rubber rain suits that kept them dry but not warm. The faster they worked, the sooner they could get out of the water and warm up. Enough of Aaron's men had volunteered that crews could rotate out of the cold river to warm up but not until the spikes and anchors were in place. As the slow process of driving the spikes began, the crew with the top plates finished. When enough of the spikes had been driven into anchor the dam, the last dam could be set in place. The plan was to start the spikes driving and support plate installations while at the same time begin pumping operations on the first. Ervin wouldn't have even considered this shortcut due to the undue safety risk if he had ample time. However, this was a time of war, and this highway was as important as any town or hill's capture would be in the coming battles. He had cleared this abbreviated method with the Ole Man.

LTC Noble having served in WW1 in France knew a thing or two about sacrifice for the greater good. He was a new second lieutenant platoon leader when his company was given the order to lead an advance on the German line. Field artillery was to begin ten minutes before his company would charge the enemy. His orders even if everything went according to the plan would result in massive losses for his men. However, other units would flank the enemy's position while his platoon would be cut to pieces. As a newly commissioned West Point Honor graduate, he had been trained to follow orders to the best of his abilities. When the time to charge came, no artillery cover fire had begun. He followed orders and led his men into well-fortified German positions. Machine gun fire began almost immediately as his platoon suffered heavy losses. The belated field artillery fire began and was falling short of the German lines, instead landing on or near his men. The only good thing that came out of the whole botched operation was the flanking units, having seen what a pounding his platoon was taking, launched a massive offensive attack. They said later that sort of unselfish sacrifice couldn't be wasted and thus inspired; they ran into the Germans' flanks that were watching the Ole Man's platoon massacre. This surprise tactic led to the killing or capturing over 560 German troops. One hundred more yards was gained that day. At the end of the battle, 2Lt Noble's platoon of 55 men sustained losses of 30 killed and 12 wounded. The Ole Man suffered fragmentation wounds from friendly field artillery fire as well as wounds from German machine gun fire. The company sustained similar losses and had to stand down. The few remaining unwounded soldiers were re-assigned to other units. 2Lt Noble spent the rest of the War in a field hospital.

While the crane operation was beginning, the pumps were operating in the first dam. The gasoline driven pump started to suck the cold river water out of the dam setup. The three-inch output hose stood straight out as if at attention as the powerful pump began to evacuate the dam's chamber. Although the pump was running at full capacity, the process would still take close to an hour. Hypothermia sets in fast in cool, wet environments especially when the wind kicks up. As if nature and the cold, harsh environment wasn't enough to cope with, the wind decided to throw another factor into the mixture.

When the conditions are right for hypothermia, it only takes a few minutes for the danger to reach a critical point. All the men in the water were Southern Colored men who had never been in a situation where they were vulnerable to hypothermia. The warning signs are only visually recognizable if you are aware of the deceptive warning signals. First, your body's core temperature starts to drop. You feel the cold, and your first instinct is to try to warm up by building a fire or moving close to a heat source. When neither of these options is realistic, then your next best option is to increase your activity. Everyone knew the temperature was in the high thirty-degree range, but nobody had any idea of the exponential effect the cold, damp, windy mixture of weather presented to the lives of the men. After ten minutes or so, the second crew whose job it was to anchor and connect the two halves of the second piling began joking about how cold they were. "Work faster and you will warm up!" shouted Aaron. All of his cold weather experience had taught him to move more and maybe stomp your feet to warm up. Like the good troops they were, they kicked it into high gear. Chills set in that made them shake uncontrollably.

"Come up for a break if you need to. We got replacements ready to dive in." Aaron said. He was beginning to get a sick feeling something bad was about to happen. Call it pride in their work, male ego, stupidity or anything else you could think of but the men wanted to finish their portion of the work.

"No Sir, Sarge. We are not cold anymore. We're just working harder to gets our ole Colored blood flowing," one of his men shouted. Since they were fired up and appeared to have beaten back the cold, Aaron reluctantly allowed him to stay in the river a while longer against his gut feeling. Hell, these ole boys are tough and know their limits. When they get cold enough, they'll come out.

What Aaron, the CO, Ervin or no one else on the job site knew was once your core temperature dropped to the low ninety-degree range, your body would start to feel warm. The shaking would stop, and you think you have beaten the cold. A euphoric and exhilarated feeling will develop misleading your brain to think you were getting warmer. The tragic fact was unless someone pulled you out of the water and warmed you up; you would die a painless death by just nodding off into your last nap.

Some mechanical malfunction had stopped the small piling driver with only one spike partially installed. The mechanic responsible for the piledriver had been sent to fix something down at the sawmill that had halted bridge timber cutting operations. The pilot as a last resort sent his last deck hand to fetch the mechanic; a fifteen-minute sojourn that would burn precious daylight, as well as leave the platform dangerously undermanned.

All that remained on board was the pilot and Aaron's men. At nearly three hundred pounds and pushing sixty, he was barely able to get himself on and off the platform without help. Aaron's highly motivated men were still inexperienced deckhands. To make matters worse, all of the men were wearing rubber suits or chest waders in anticipation of their cold water river duties. Even though this was essential equipment for normal operations, the rubber waders and suits would be sure death if they had to jump into the river to swim.

The stage was set for bad things to happen. The platform pilot, Aaron, the CO, and Ervin were all holding their breath hoping nothing out of the ordinary would happen. The men inside the second dam were beginning to act funny and caught the attention of Aaron. They had almost stopped their work; one couldn't pick up his hammer and spikes. The other man was laughing but in a voice and tone of a drunkard. This behavior was new territory for Aaron. He didn't know what was wrong, but he had to do something fast. As luck would have it, the boat used to ferry the men was on the bank since the deckhand had used it to fetch the mechanic. Swimming the twenty feet to the second dam site would be a doable task in the warm Tombigbee River, but this was not that ole slow warm river Aaron remembered. Aaron tied a rope around his waist and told his men to hold on to the rope. He signaled the pilot and jumped into the frigid water of the Sikanna Chief River; one of the coldest fastest flowing rivers in Canada. As Aaron disappeared below the water's surface, the sudden cold took his breath away. Almost as an involuntary reflex, Aaron opened his mouth for a big breath of air. Of course all he sucked in was cold river water. Aaron panicked and started to pull on the rope. Luckily for Aaron, his men were paying attention and pulled him to the surface and back to the deck. Aaron was throwing up everything in his stomach at the same time trying to expel the water in his lungs. After a minute or so, Aaron was ready to go back into the water on his second attempt to rescue his men.

The last few minutes had focused everyone's attention on Aaron and his rescue attempt. Nobody had seen the serious threat floating downstream toward the platform. As is common in these rivers, trees uprooted by rain and the wind will end up in a river floating downstream. Some of these trees are forty to sixty feet tall (or long now) and have the roots, and most of its branches still attached. The mass of the water soaked tree combined with the velocity of the river translates into one hell of a battering ram ready to move most anything in its path. The engineers had designed the piling structure to withstand these normal occurrences, but all that was holding the first piling dam was five or six spikes of the twenty designed to anchor it to the riverbed. A great deal of the water had been pumped out of the structure that meant the force of the river current was now putting more pressure on the structure greater than it was when it was full of water. The second dam was in far greater danger. None of the anchor spikes had been driven into the timbers; only the connecting plates designed to marry the two halves. The tree barreling down the river would collide with both of the dams, and only one would remain anchored. The other dam most likely would stop the tree briefly, only to have it slowly lift the dam up off the river bed allowing the current to flow under and into the water chamber. Aaron's men with hypothermia were helplessly heading toward a slow death. Heaven only knows what would happen. Still, with everybody's full undivided attention focused on Aaron's rescue attempt, the danger heading in their direction continued its steady and deadly journey.

Aaron had expelled the water from his burning lungs but was undeterred in his attempt to save his men. The CO and Ervin stood on the river banks helpless as they watched this heroic attempt by Aaron. Their sole consolation was the best man in the unit was in the water, and nothing more could be done. This rescue would be over regardless of the results in a couple of minutes. The CO and Ervin both being raised in a cold weather climate had seen or heard about this condition. No one had a name for it, but they had seen this sort of thing before. Both were worried Aaron would succumb to the condition before he could reach the men.

Aaron swam as he had never swum before cutting through the swift river current like an Olympic contestant. He reached the structure just as one of the men let go and disappeared below the water. "Damnit, Trooper, you are not dying on my watch. I have already lost too many men so far." Aaron had swum to the upstream side of the dam so the current could assist him in climbing over the walls. As he reached the wall, a welcomed wave lifted him up and over the wall. He quickly told the other man to hold on while he attempted to locate the man that had just disappeared. Aaron reached down into the back of the dam's wall near the bottom and felt the collar of his man. He struggled to lift both his weight and his man up to the surface. Somehow he managed to lift his man's head above the water as he came back from was certain death. He opened his eyes and spat out some water. He was alive but just barely. Aaron tied his lifeline on the nearly dead man. The other trooper was in better shape since he was making fun of his buddy. Having lifted the guy over the wall, Aaron signaled to the men on the platform to pull fast. Aaron had no idea how he would get the rope back. The men from the first dam were safely on the platform by now. They were cold but alive and grateful to be out of the cold river.

They pulled the semiconscious man onto the deck. Just then, one of the men looked upstream not fifty yards from the dams and platform's location, saw a massive tree as wide as the river thundering toward all of them. He screamed at the top of his lungs, "Jesus Christ, there's a big tree coming at us."

The pilot had but one maneuver. The pilot thought if he positioned the platform upstream, he could dampen the full force by letting the tree dissipate some of its energy on the boat's platform before it hit the dam. The maneuver might work if the engine doesn't stall. There was no way as big and long as this tree was that he could save the dam.

"Stow the anchor and prepare for a collision. Hold on to something, men."

"No time to tell anybody about my plan. Hell, he thought to himself, I don't know for sure myself what I am going to do."

The pilot maneuvered the platform quickly into position to block the tree as best he could. With any luck, the platform would take the brunt of the force. The tree was longer than the platform, but not heavier. The platform had more tonnage or so the skipper thought. The only fault in this plan was the tree was moving at a speed of a glacier-fed river current, and the platform was stationary. No time to pull the slide rule out, this will be over one way or the other in less than a minute. Every day we waste hours upon hours just doing nothing. It's only when you have but one minute possibly left in your life does seconds become precious. In this situation, all on board the platform didn't need to be told what to do. One of the men pulled the nearly dead man into the center of the deck and attempted to lash him down. One of the other men quickly tied a big wrench to the rope, hollered to Aaron to get his attention and tossed him his lifeline. The line hit Aaron right in the chest. Aaron was noticing his hands and feet were feeling like they had ten pound Martha White flour bags tied to each of them. His man on the line noticed Aaron was reacting and talking more slowly than earlier. He was afraid his sergeant was getting whatever the other two had done got. The other two men were busy saving their butts instead of pitching in to save Aaron and their pals. One's true character becomes evident in these types of situations. It doesn't take a genius to figure out which ones you would want to be with you in a foxhole.

It was a race to save two men and the bridge project. The pilot was a civilian but had served in WW1 as had his two brothers, one of which had been buried in France. He had a son and a nephew in the Navy in the Pacific, and he was fighting in this war too. The platform reached its position just seconds before impact. Time had frozen for Aaron, who was beginning to feel the effects of the cold as had his men. He had managed to tie the line around the other trooper who was still conscience but was losing his motor skills. This man had less than a couple of minutes before he would lose his battle and die. Time was ticking away by the second. Aaron could not appreciate the gravity of his situation. He was getting tunnel vision, and his thought process was being to be severely retarded by the second. He, however, knew his man needed to be lifted over the wall now if he was to have any chance of survival. Aaron mustered all his strength and willpower to heave the man over the wall as his buddy on the deck pulled him on the platform only seconds before impact. In those scant seconds, the trooper turned deckhand pulled his barely alive friend onto the deck's center just with enough time to lash him down. The only man in the water was Aaron. Time had run out for his rescue.

"Grab whole of something, NOW!" yelled the pilot as the tree that looked as big as a barn collided with the platform. The next few seconds were in slow motion if you were on board the platform. As the pilot had planned, the tree hit his platform and turned into a more parallel path as it moved downstream.

Hell, thought the pilot, we might just live through this, after all.

The big tree's momentum had been partially dissipated by the pilot's action but not entirely. This vessel was not designed to maneuver with the force needed totally push such a large tree away from the dam. Just when most the pilot thought the worst was over, disaster struck. The overwhelming force of the trees mass and the current overcame the capabilities of both the pilot and his vessel. As soon as the short-lived celebration began, it ended. In a split second, the tree swung around trunk first with all the roots and branches still attached. A huge collection of root ball and limbs hit the platform square in the wheelhouse. This small compartment was nothing but a thin wood box designed to keep the pilot dry in a rainstorm. The tree's big root ball hit the wheelhouse with such force; it carried the pilot and the entire wheelhouse into the river. The collision caused the engine to die which was all that was keeping the platform and the tree away from the dam. For Aaron, his only hope of survival was to try and grab onto the deck. Maybe on some other day, this might have worked but today was not one of those days. Before Aaron could move to make an attempt to save himself, the tree pushed the vessel into the dam. The action lifted the dam up and allowed the swift, deadly cold Sikanna Chief River water to wash him downstream. The last the men saw of Aaron was him bobbing up and down as he disappeared around the bend of the river. On the platform, the men on the deck were feverously trying to save themselves and their fellow soldiers. Karma has a way of rewarding good and punishing evil. The two men that saved their asses and didn't lift a finger to help the rest had been swept overboard in the collision. The wreck wasn't over yet. Without engine power, the platform began to float rudderless downstream along with the tree. Debris and equipment from the vessel covered the entire river from bank to bank. By now almost everyone at the site was racing to the rescue of the men in peril. The first pair to assist was the CO and Ervin, who had already manned the small flat bottom boat used to ferry the men to the platform and the banks. The 25 horsepower Johnson outboard motor fired up and was headed to the runaway vessel. The remaining men still on deck were racing to attach as many rope and line as they could to the anything possible on the platform. A quick thinking sawmill worker had fired up one of the big tractors and was headed to the bank downstream. Two other men had jumped on the back with a 100-foot length of chain. They secured the chain to the drawbar and were ready to toss the end to the deckhands. Fortunately for the crew, the platform was not floating as fast as the current which enabled the crew on the tractor to drive into the river in time to throw the chain to the men. They immediately lashed it to a dead man welded into the deck after taking up some of the slack. The fast thinking on both the parts of the sawmill crew and the troops saved the platform as the big tractor pulled the vessel on the bank and to a stop.

The CO and Ervin were looking for any survivors in the river. The old pilot who had been so violently launched from the deck somehow had made it to the bank. Several of the soldiers were in the water helping him out. He was upright and walking by the grace of God. The two men from the river were beginning to show signs that the effects of hypothermia were subsiding. A quick headcount revealed three men were still unaccounted for and presumed to be still in the grip of the river current. The CO and Ervin yelled to the men on the banks to run as fast as could downstream to look for Aaron and the two other men while they pointed the boat downstream. It seemed Karma had paid the other two men a visit even earlier in the day. These two men were not the best workers in Colored Camp. As a matter of fact, the men had given them nicknames; Sick and Slack. They were always in the chow and sick call line first. If there were a choice between an easy job and one more important, you could bet your butt these two would pick the jobs that took the least amount of effort. Not bad men; likable enough but you couldn't depend on them in a jam. Earlier in the day when given a choice between full rubber suits and chest waders, they took the chest wader. They had overheard Ervin tell Aaron the men in the chest waders should only be sent in the water as a last resort. Of course, if they had hung around to listen to why he had made that suggestion, they might have made a better choice. While the chest waders were easier to wear and work in, the downside was if you fell into the river, unlike the full rubber suits, the chest waders would fill up with water immediately. They would be like a parachute for water that would most likely suck you in the water to your death. If these two had bad Karma, then Aaron Park had an abundance of good Karma stored.

The rescue effort would continue until everyone was found, dead or alive. By now close to a hundred men were involved in the effort. The CO and Ervin were ahead of the men on foot hoping to find Aaron and the other men safe on the banks of the river. Unknown to them around the bend in the river was a wide delta of many small channels. This flat open area extended miles across from the river bank to river bank instead of the few hundred yards back at the bridge crossing site. Large open gravel banks separated these many channels. Some could be navigated, and some just dead ended requiring valuable daylight to retrace their routes to areas more likely to yield survivors. Neither the CO nor Ervin would say out loud what they were thinking; this was quickly becoming a recovery rather than a rescue mission. Ervin had never lost anyone close to him; neither a family member or a close friend. For some reason, this young Colored man from Mississippi had made an impression on him he would not soon forget. He had witnessed a true act of heroism to save two friends without regard for his life. Aaron Park had made sure two of his men were safe before he tried to make it to safety. Time had run out for the young sergeant from the 95th Colored Engineer Regiment. The tree had taken his last chance of rescue away before he was swept downstream to an almost certain cold watery grave. Not the ending this man deserved; he should have made it through this war, married and raised some wonderful kids he and his wife would have been proud of. Life is not fair. The only good thing the men had going for them was they had enough men to search the whole river delta before dark. A very small chance remained for the three if they were located before darkness fell. Death would be certain if they weren't found before the temperature dropped and the bears and wolf packs came out to hunt for supper.

Back at the river crossing, the pilot was barking orders out like a drill sergeant. He was determined to get the platform back into duty back by morning. By some stroke of luck (something in damn short supply around Colored Camp), the steering and throttle mechanisms were fixable. His cozy little wheelhouse was now a 150-pound keg of nails, and his maple and brass steering wheel was now a cross made from rough-cut two by two lumber supplied by the sawmill. Any port in a storm as the seafarers saying goes. The only parts that could have grounded them for the winter if broken were the shaft and propeller. Of all the sticks and stones that could have bent or broken these two vital parts, all had been missed. They were ready for duty. The pile driver mechanic was on board with orders not to leave until both the pile drivers were ready for action. For all the crap floating around the vessel in the river, none was vital to the operation. It seemed the tree had not done as much damage as it could have.

In a war, your brain has the wonderful quality to segregate information into compartments so you can work on one task without having something on your mind. All the workers were feverously slaving away on the platform while three of their own were likely dead. Sick and Slack were lazy screw-ups, but they all liked them. They just knew not to get between those two and a fried pork chop. But Sergeant Aaron Park was different. He had been their rock since leaving the place they had called home and had guided them through all the hard times. No one else could fill that void.

CHAPTER 13

THE AWAKENING

"Aaron, Aaron. Wake your lazy butt up." Rose said to him.

What a wonderful dream it was. Rose was shaking him from a little nap on the front porch, and as his eyes opened, he could see her smiling face.

"Sorry Rose, I must have dozed off after all that fried chicken, mashed potatoes and gravy you made for dinner. It sure was good."

"Rose, who the Hell is Rose, "n....r." Wake up Damnit. You can't pass on just yet." yelled one of Aaron's men.

"Captain Taylor, we found him over there; he's alive but saying something crazy about a rose."

Captain Taylor and Ervin opened up the throttle all the way and got the flat bottom boat up on step as they raced over to the recovery site. It was a gravel bar big enough for Wiley to have landed his Piper J-3 Cub separating them and the men. It would be quicker to have them bring him over than try to find the most direct route to the channel. Before they even got to the bank, the rescue crew was already toting Aaron over. They gingerly put Aaron in the boat with one of the men and the four roared back up river to the work site. In a few short minutes, they arrived. All the men could hear all three men yelling, "We found Aaron, we found Aaron, and he's alive!"

A party of fellow soldiers was waiting to assist with Aaron's transfer to the medical tent. The Doc was already at the site to check him out. The men had made five beds in a heated makeshift hospital for the survivors. The two men rescued by Aaron were in recovery and doing well. They quickly carried Aaron, who was still not fully awake. They doubted he knew where he was, but he had the best attention possible now. Doc told the Co and Ervin his blood pressure was low as well as his temperature. He started an IV drip and cranked the heat up high. The next couple of hours would tell the tale if Aaron would recover.

Things were under control given the events of the afternoon at the bridge construction site. It was hard to imagine all of the damage and injuries had occurred in less than two minutes. One minute, everything was going great and then BOOM; things went to hell.

The search continued for the two missing men, Sick and Slack. Most of the men on rescue duty knew that the chance of finding them alive was slim, but they had to go on looking as if they were still alive. As they worked their way across the delta of Sikanna Chief River, a heavy mood filled their hearts. Sure, they lost people before, but Sick and Slack were pretty good old boys and didn't deserve to die like this. With any luck, they would find them before dark, but the prospect for a happy ending was diminishing exponentially. The sun goes down early this time of year in the far

north. Bad things happen after dark; predators come out to feed
and don't care what species their supper is. It makes no difference
to them where they kill him a moose and caribou or a kid from the
village; it's all just food for them. Two dead or nearly dead Colored
boys from Mississippi would be easy picking. Most of the men silently
searching thought that it would probably be better if they were dead
by sundown if their fate were going to be supper for a pack of wolves.

While the search was going on downstream in the river
delta, repairs were being made to the platform barge so the bridge
construction project could get back underway. The scene was one of
controlled chaos. The sawmill was back in the full-scale production
cutting and preserving the main timbers so they'd be ready for the
pile driving part of the project. Many timbers were yet to be sawn and
positioned for this project. Repairs on the barge platform are moving
along ahead of schedule. The CO and Mr. Swanson were in awe at
the coordinated effort of the whole team. Colored Camp was in full
swing and running at peak performance in light of the circumstances.

Meanwhile, in the medic tent, efforts to pull Aaron through
this critical phase were proceeding although not much more could
be accomplished with the limited staff and equipment available.
Aaron's full recovery depended on his inner strength and will to
live. He was in a coma and dreaming about Rose, the life he hoped
to live with her, the kids he would raise with her in Chicago. No
sir nowhere in his dreams was there any room for cotton fields, hay
barns and no white ass boss man back in Mississippi. Aaron had
only been gone from Mississippi a little less than a year, but that part
of his life seemed like a distant memory. No Sir, there would be no
more fried gizzards and chicken backs, red eye gravy in his future.
You could be certain for damn sure no more grits or chitlins (fried,
boiled or stump slung) would be on the menu for this Colored man

in Chi-Town. Aaron's dream of Rose and his life in Chicago had brought an unconscious smile to his face; that fact had brought hope to the medical staff that Aaron would pull through. His vital signs were still critical and guarded, but at least he had stabilized and only time will tell if he would wake up and live the remainder of his life as in his dream. A 24 hour a day watch was on Aaron. All the men had volunteered to take an eight-hour shift after their long duty day, but the CO said no. The men would get at least 10 hours rest, and other arrangements had been made to assure Sgt. Park' care was the best possible. What the men of Colored Camp didn't realize was that the arrangements that they had made included the CO and Mr. Swanson and some of the other men from the mill.

The sun had finally sunk below the Canadian Rocky Mountains, and darkness had fallen on the camp. Men were still out searching for Sick and Slack. The CO was just about to shut down the search because the danger was too great for men to be out there unarmed at night even in numbers that topped more than ninety troopers. The CO got in the boat along with a couple of others armed with rifles and headed down the river just in case there were bears or wolves. The men were tired, cold, and wet, but they weren't ready to stop. Knowing their two brothers in arms were out there somewhere possibly having their body devoured by wild animals gave them strength to soldier on into the cold darkness. As the CO pulled up to the beach near the biggest group of searchers, Specialist Fourth (Spec 4) Class Wilson greeted him.

"Sir we searched all but about 10% of this area. We have all talked about it and if it's okay with you, Sir; we would like to proceed with the rescue at least another hour. We think we know the area that they probably are. We are all tired, wet and hungry, but if a slim chance Sick or Slack are alive, then we owe it to them to find them tonight."

The old man did not hesitate. He looked at Specialist Fourth Class Wilson and the rest his men and said

"Soldier on."

Back at camp, the repair on the platform barge was going smooth as could be expected. It was dark and cold in the middle of the Canadian wilderness. Working with the metal tools on the steel deck barge was made more difficult with the drop in temperature and high humidity. The hypothermia experienced by the people in the water earlier was now felt by everyone working on the crew. Some had the rubber chest high boots on and were partially in the water. The men working on the steel deck were feeling their hands swell to what felt like the size of a big snapping turtle. Not the little turtles that climb up on a log to sun but the big bad ass ones that just sticks their heads out of the water.

Everybody had Captain Bob, the platform pilot, pegged as a lazy ass old white man with a good job. The skipper's 300 pounds gave people the notion that all he was able to do was set on his big lard ass in the pilot house and move some levers. Well, looks can be deceiving, and they were. Capt. Bob Garrett carried his 300 pounds around like he weighed 110 pounds. He was a man driven as if God inspired him. The men working on his platform didn't know that he had served in World War I. Also he had a brother that died during the First World War on the Western front and had a son and a nephew that was serving in the Navy right now. Colored Camp had a lot of respect for Capt. Bob now and all he had to do was say jump, and they just asked how high. The repair on the barge platform was only a few hours away from being complete. Captain Bob released half his men on the barge and told them to go back and get some sleep. The men that remained were all volunteers and wanted to see the repair through to the end. They said they could sleep after they got this bridge built.

In the hospital tent, the entire staff and the CO were closely monitoring Sgt. Park' progress. The young but capable medic told them that Sgt. Park' critical time would be between now and sunup. His core temperature, blood pressure, and heart rate was better but still well below normal. The wait would have to continue a while longer.

Rose looked as his pretty as she'd ever looked. Aaron always liked the way Rose looked when she put on one of those bright sundresses she and her mom bought in downtown Chicago. Yes, Sir, a Colored man or woman could walk right into any store and buy something just like white folks in Chicago.

Aaron's sons and daughter were playing on the floor of the living room. Aaron was a proud Dad. Just think how good life will be for his kids and grandkids he thought. Rose and her Mom were in the kitchen fixing supper while he and granddaddy watched the kids. The White Sox's had a home game playing on the radio and the Cubs, well who in the hell cares.

Yes, life was good for Aaron Park. Scooter Park, the field hand, was dead. Aaron Park was much alive and living in Chicago. Suddenly a black cloud covered the sky. His father-in-law had disappeared as well as two of his kids. Only the oldest boy was still there. But something was terribly wrong because his son was older and covered with blood. Aaron tried to get up and go to him, but he couldn't. The boy screamed in agony and pain as he looked at his father. Aaron world was coming apart in front of his eyes. He yelled as loud as he could as the boy faded away. The pain a father feels when one of his children is sick or dying is immeasurable. Aaron screamed as loud as he could as his first born son faded out of view.

"Sgt. Park wake up! You're having a nightmare."

Aaron awoke and set straight up in the bed. He was covered in sweat, and his blood pressure was above normal. The medic and the CO grabbed him by the shoulders.

"Sgt. Park, wake up. We were worried about you, and we're all glad that you're okay."

The CO sent a runner out to tell the men that Sgt. Park was out of danger and would be back on duty in a few days.

"Sgt. Park, you had some nightmare. Do you remember anything about your dream?"

Oh yes, Aaron remembered everything, but he was not about to tell anyone especially, Rose. He didn't understand how his brain could play such a sick joke on him. But he didn't want to understand a dream that took one of his kids they haven't even had yet away in such a violent manner. Analyzing that dream was above his pay grade. It was just a stupid dream and meant nothing.

But something told Aaron it portended of something terrible to come. This dream was Aaron's little secret, and no one would ever know.

"I don't remember anything about my dream. The last thing I remember was being in the water and being swept downstream. I got cold started shivering but then the shivering stopped, and I warmed up. After that, I drifted off to sleep. The next thing I remember was one of the men shaking me and telling me to wake up."

The CO looked at Aaron and said,

"Well, you had us worried for a while, Trooper. Do you remember anything you did?"

"No sir, the whole thing is a blur. I just remember bits and pieces of it. I vaguely remember the big tree hitting the platform. I remember jumping in the water with a rope to try to rescue two of my men who are acting funny. After that Sir, I just remember waking up just now. Are my men okay?"

"Sgt. Park, you were a hero today. At least two men are alive, thanks to you. Those two men you rescued are fine and back at work. However, Sick and Slack were swept downstream and hadn't been found. I'm holding out little hope for their rescue. Almost everyone that is not working on the barge is on the rescue team. I gave them an additional hour to try to find them. That was about 45 minutes ago so they should be showing back up anytime. I didn't feel comfortable leaving them out there after dark any longer."

Specialist Wilson and his rescue team were searching the last stretch of river for the two missing man. The marksmen that had been issued weapons were leading the search party when they suddenly stopped, signaled with their hand for the search party to stop and crouch down on one knee. Down the river on one of the gravel beaches in that flat river delta silhouetted against the Canadian moon was a very big grizzly bear. The bear's attention appeared to be occupied by something on the ground. All the men could see the bear. That meant since they were upwind of the bear it would only be a matter of time before the bear would see them. To a bear, the ninety men look like a big bunch of moose calves and not a unit of soldiers on humanitarian search and rescue mission. An eight foot nine-hundred pound grizzly bear can sprint up to thirty-five miles an hour and is capable of taking any prey it desires. From fifty yards away the grizzly bear could be on the entire unit in less than a minute, and the stampede that would follow would be just what the bear wanted. Since none of the men are capable of running thirty-five miles an hour and there is always somebody that the slowest in the bunch, it's a foregone conclusion that the bear will catch at least one soldier. Having exchanged silent hand signals, the marksmen took a bead on the grizzly bear fifty yards downriver. Mere seconds later shots rang out, and the grizzly bear that once posed an imminent danger to the unit lay dead on its side. As they walked up to the site, a horrible scene unfolded. The reason the bear had not spotted or smelled them was that the bear had already found Sick and Slack and was eating their dead bodies. The lead soldier signaled the men to stop. Wilson and the marksmen agreed it was best not to tell them about the bear eating their two friends. The search party was ordered back to the camp. Wilson and the marksmen field dressed the bear, put the remains of Sick and Slack in the boat with the bear meat and hide then headed back to camp. The rest the night was uneventful, and the citizens of Colored Camp were happy the previous tragic day was over. They had lost two of their own and an irreplaceable day of construction time. But everyone else was fine including their leader, Sgt. Aaron Park. The men never knew that the bear had partly eaten Sick and Slack. Instead, they enjoyed bear sausage at chow the next morning. Specialist Wilson and the marksman passed on the bear meat telling the men that they felt the search and rescue team deserved the meat more.

Some secrets should go to the grave, and this was one of those.

Things were back to normal at the construction site. The cold front had stalled and would not reach them for days. The pilings installation went without a hitch; no more trees cascading down the river, or hungry grizzly bears. As day three ended, the Arctic storm had slowed down enough to give the crew an extra day or two before the winter freeze. Capt. Bob was at the control of the platform barge with both pile drivers in good working order. They managed to drive in the spikes that anchored the dams in place on both pilings, started to pump the water from the inside and were almost finished by dark. Mr. Swenson decided to call it a day so the men could use some good rest. Aaron was still under the medic's care although he said he was ready for duty. The medic and the CO said NO and that was final. They both agreed however that tomorrow he would probably be released from medical care and would be able to return to his duties with his men.

Day four began very early long before sunup. The impending cold front was still advancing their way, and you could see the clouds in the distance as they began to gather. Everyone knew what this meant as soon as the clouds got over them it would be colder, and it would be some precipitation none of which were favorable to bridge building. All that remained to be finished was the 24 inch x 18 inch x 30 foot treated timbers to be sunk in the riverbed, coupled together, and rocks piled in around them. The engineers had come up with a plan would require all the men, the platform barge, and all the small boats to coordinate to ensure that these pilings were

positioned correctly. The men awoke to the pounding sound of the
pile drivers clearing out pilot holes to set the timbers. These holes
were 10 feet into the riverbed. The timbers would then be lowered
into the hole; the engineers would ensure that the timbers were plumb
before river rock was put into the hole and packed down. This step
would be done on all four double timber pilings before the pile driver
started. A metal cap made from 8 gauge Pittsburg steel had been
installed to prevent splintering. When the first pile driver was began
to pound, it made so much noise the men were sure Colored men
in the cotton fields of the Mississippi Delta could hear the sound.
This loud banging marked the beginning of the end of the 95th
Colored Engineer Regiment's mission in Alaska and Canada. This
life changing journey had begun at Camp Shelby, Mississippi almost
a year ago soon after the Japs attacked Pearl Harbor. The six-week
layover for training in Chicago changed Aaron's life when he met the
future Mrs. Rose Park. Stick a fork in it; this highway was close to
an end (at least this construction project). The CO had told Aaron
the unit would be dissolved and sent to different areas of operation.
Orders would be issued at the completion ceremony in a few weeks,
and not even the Ole Man knew what they contained.

It was never a good idea to plan too far ahead in the Army, so
Aaron stuck to the task at hand. As Erwin had said, after the pilings
were in, the actual bridge construction would go quickly. The men at
the sawmill had cut and stacked more than enough timbers for this
and half of another bridge. All hands were on deck, and a friendly
intra-unit completion was in full swing.

You could see and hear the bulldozers finishing the remaining
segment of the 1500 plus mile Alcan Highway. The importance
of this highway to the war effort would be hard to overstate. This
road would be used to supply fuel for the delivery of our Russian

allies' fighters and bombers to help defeat Hilter. A big stage and bleachers were under construction as the last few timbers were spiked into place. The 95th had asked Erwin to drive in the last spike, and he proudly honored their request. A small handwritten sign with all the men's names and hometown that had given their lives for the project was nailed to the underside of the bridge. It was no way General Jefferson would ever allow any recognition of the 95th Colored Engineer Regiment. Karma, however, would have a way of making things right. The General had managed to piss some of the citizen soldiers who were politically connected to the men in power in Washington. Instead of commanding a combat unit in battle under General George Patton, he would instead spend the rest of the war and his career as garrison commander at Big Delta Army Air Field at Delta Junction, Alaska. Ironically, the racist asshole General Jefferson would end up in what officers called a terminal assignment in wartime at an Army Air Field in charge of essentially nothing but a few hangers, snow plows, and the runway. The Army captain in command of the aviation unit on the airfield could pick up the phone and inform General Jefferson the runway needed plowing.

A giant but deserved step down for the General who could tell his grandchildren when asked, "What did you do in the great war, Grandpappy?"

"Well, I shoved snow in Alaska." He could say sheepishly.

A convoy of Army vehicles loaded with fuel and supplies for the Army garrison in Alaska was lined up ready to cross over the Sikanna Chief River Bridge. The temperature was 10 degrees that sunless November day in British Columbia, Canada. The Army had photographers from the Signal Corp taking pictures of General Jefferson giving now Colonel Noble and newly promoted

Major Taylor a unit citation for the outstanding job the 95th Colored
Engineer Regiment had done. The award had been delivered to
the General at the same time as his new assignment orders with
instructions to present the award in person as his last official act as
Alaskan Commander. Following the ribbon cutting, he would assume
the post of Garrison Commander at Delta Junction, Alaska.

Aaron was awarded an Army Achievement Medal for his
outstanding service to the project. Aaron could barely hold his
laughter inside when the grandson of a Confederate slave-owning
General had to shake his hand and congratulate him, a Colored boy
from Mississippi, for his service. ***Man, life is great.*** Aaron and the
rest of the 95th had no idea where the General was going to spend the
rest of the war and couldn't care less. As long as the son of a bitch
kept his racist ass out of their business, he could go anywhere he
wanted.

With the completion of the Alcan Highway, the 95th Colored
Engineer Regiment was to be dissolved, and members sent to various
units destined for overseas theaters of operation. A good portion of
the men was sent to the newly formed Colored construction unit in
New Orleans, Louisiana while most of the rest of the soldiers received
orders to the European or the Pacific theater of operation. Aaron
and a few of his best men from the 95th received orders to report
Camp Atterbury; a new training installation in Indiana for a unit
assignment to be determined at a later date. To Aaron's surprise, he
had been granted a 30-day leave en route to Camp Atterbury. Aaron
knew what he was going to do on his leave. When he reported for
duty at Camp Atterbury, he would be sporting a new wedding band.

"Sergeant Park," said Major Taylor after all the men had
received orders.

"Yes Sir," Aaron replied.

"Come over for a minute, please." As Aaron approached his CO, he noticed a tan military looking envelope in the CO's hand. Major Taylor returned Aaron's salute as he reported and said,

"Sgt. Park, I've got something else for you before you leave. I called in a favor and got you on a train here in British Columbia which after a few changes of transportation will have you in Chicago two weeks before Christmas. I hope I didn't overstep my bounds."

"Hell no, I mean No Sir, sorry Sir." Exclaimed Aaron in a voice so loud almost everyone turned to look.

"Thank you, Sir, Thank you.

CHAPTER 14

HOMECOMING AND WEDDING BELLS

Rose had been planning a homecoming party just in case Aaron got leave on his way overseas. Her parents had told her to offer Aaron the use of the spare bedroom for his leave (and her wedding, they prayed). The building and completion of the Alaska Highway had been in the newspaper for weeks. Rose had proudly told everyone she knew her boyfriend was helping build that road. She couldn't have been prouder. Aaron hadn't told her of his near death experience in the river or the wolf attack on one of his men. That attack had been a war experience and the women folk didn't need to hear all the details. Aaron would tell his future father-in-law about the encounters and Mr. Porter was glad Aaron had exercised such good judgment.

The church basement had a big community room Rose could use for the party if and when Aaron got time to visit her. The last letters Rose got were over two months old when she received them so Aaron could be anywhere. Little did she know her future husband would be calling her soon with the long awaited news of his arrival.

Aaron was on the train that would eventually get him to Chicago and his beloved Rose. The familiar clack of the train wheels was a reminder of how far he had come from that cotton patch in North Mississippi. Aaron was now a decorated sergeant in the United States Army on his way to fight Japs or Nazis for God and Country. He had always been on the side of God but fighting for a country that allowed people to be treated differently just because of the color of their skin was new to this old Colored country boy. Aaron had found that Colored folks received better treatment the further north you traveled and that fact meant the world to him. Rose and Aaron would raise their kids where the white devil didn't rule so help him, God.

After the train had cleared US customs, the conductor told everyone the train would be at the station for 45 minutes before departing for Chicago. Aaron jumped up out of his seat and ran into the terminal looking for a phone booth.

Being in Alaska had one of the benefits Aaron hadn't planned on; payday was in cash. Since Aaron didn't gamble or drink, he had saved all his money to buy Rose a big wedding ring. The last three paydays were paid at the end of the project due to some transportation issue with the payroll. The bottom line was he had a wad of cash big enough to choke a mule. Aaron had never felt richer. He thought this is how the white folks feel in the fall after they had sold their fall crops. Talk about walking in high cotton my ass; this was like flying over them damn ole cotton fields.

After getting enough nickels and dimes to call and talk to Rose for a day, Aaron pulled the piece of paper with Rose's folk's telephone number on it and dialed the number. The operator said deposit $1.10 please, and Aaron put 11 dimes in that black and chrome Ma Bell phone faster than lighting. The phone rang and rang and rang so long Aaron was afraid he wouldn't be able to talk to her until he arrived in Chicago. He had pulled that piece of paper out of his billfold so many times during his tour in Alaska; he had memorized the number; Rosedale 254. He would rub his finger over the numbers Rose had written and remembered the day she gave it to him right before he departed. The blue wool dress she wore on that dreary day would pop into his mind. Her last kiss on his cheek was vividly burned into his brain. Gone for a second was the cold hard, miserable, working conditions outside, and a calm, pleasant mood would overwhelm him. But being a sergeant in charge meant somebody was always looking for you. Eventually, his out of body experience would be broken by, "Sarge, we need you out here."

After what seemed like an eternity someone finally picked up the phone and said,

"Hello."

"Rose, this is Aaron. How are you Honey Child?"

Aaron had called Rose Honey Child, Sweetie Pie and several other foreign terms Rose had never heard before. The terms were new to her; she knew if her man wanted her to be his Honey Child then she would be his honey child. Those bees better get ready to make all the honey they could because she was going to be the sweetest Honey Child living in the Windy City.

"Aaron," she screamed into the phone, so loud everyone in the house came to see what the problem was.

"It's okay Mama; Aaron's on the phone." The first time she had heard Aaron's voice in 10 months was a blessing for which she had prayed for months.

"Sweetheart, I am so glad to hear from you. Where are you?"

What she wanted to know was when I will see you. Her father had warned her soldiers in times of war seldom are allowed leave en route to a combat zone. The policy is due to higher desertion rate of new soldiers headed to battle zones for the first time.

"Honey, I'm on a train headed to Chicago to see you. We are at the US-Canadian border and will on the way in a half hour. I have 30 days leave en route to a place called Camp Atterbury, Indiana. I can't wait to see you. As soon as I find a place to stay I will come over."

"You listen to me Aaron Park, Sergeant in the US Army. Our home is your home, and I will be at the train station to pick you up."

"Yes Um," Aaron said very wisely for the first of many times in his coming life with Rose.

CHAPTER 15

UNION TRAIN STATION CHI-TOWN

Early December 1942

Rose's Dad had driven Rose to the train station so she and Aaron could catch up in the back seat on the way home. Rose's Dad had called an old friend from the local ward that was a big Dawg at the railroad. He gave his friend the place and time Aaron had called. Within a half hour, he called back with the status and time of his arrival. Rose's Dad old buddy cut through red tape to get the time, but when Rose's Dad told how special this passenger was, his buddy had the Red Caps ready to take his luggage to a special parking spot outside the door reserved for dignitaries. A Colored man in uniform decorated by a General who helped build the road to Alaska was a hero. Little did they know how true a hero he was!

Aaron had been asking the Colored conductor "are we there yet" for hours. The Colored man was a gentleman and gave Aaron a minute by minute update whenever Aaron asked him. The two of them had had long talks about Aaron's Army service, his life as a Colored man growing up in Mississippi and his plans with Rose. The Colored man had to be excused from time to time so he could shed a tear in private. You see, his wife of 54 years had passed less than a year before. Aaron's story reminded him of those early days when his heart hurt so badly when they were apart. He had started with the railroad company when he was young because the train went all the way to New Orleans where the passengers were segregated by race. No white conductor would serve Colored passengers. That sort of thing just wasn't done; union rules don't you know. It was okay for a Colored man to serve white folks because God had intended for man (white men) to have dominion over the creatures of the earth (which according to most Southern Baptist preachers included Colored folks).

Henry, the Colored conductor, had benefited from this rule since he could cover all passenger cars. Henry remembered just how he felt the closer he got to home. Aaron's story reminded him of all those years of wonderful love and bliss with his departed wife, Bess. Nowadays he just as soon stay on the train than to go to his home filled with all those memories.

Talking to Aaron about Rose and their plans uplifted the ole man and made him realize that the circle of life would not be broken. Finally, Henry was grateful for his time he had had with Bess; his lovely recently departed wife. Their four grown children all had families of their own now. Henry now knew Bess would want him to enjoy his time left on earth with their flock because they would be united once again for eternity in heaven.

It seemed Aaron had a quality that sort rubbed off on those he met. This rare attribute would serve him well in the future.

"Hurry, Daddy, Aaron's train will be there before us. He'll think I am not picking him up and might go to a hotel or something." Rose yelled at her father.

The ole man just smiled remembering when he and her Mom were young and in love, how important every minute together was and how a day apart seemed like an eternity.

"Rose, we will be at the station thirty minutes before the train even clears the city limits so settle down."

"Daddy, I'm sorry but the closer we get to the station, the more I miss him. Where you and Mom like this when you were in college and apart all week?" Rose said to her father.

The ole man had to tell his daughter the truth.

"Rose, I believe your Mom and I were worse than you and Aaron. I would pack my bags on Thursday night so I could leave right after my last class. The train ride only took two hours, but it seemed like six. I remember thinking can't this pile of iron go faster? Doesn't the conductor know how important it is for me to get home? Yes, Baby Girl, I know just how you feel. But don't you dare tell your Mama I said that because I always played it cool."

Those words from her Daddy made Rose feel good. She had always known her parents were in love but to know how deeply in love they were was a comfort to her. She and Aaron were going to be just like her parents. That's not a bad role model for a young couple in love in the 1940's.

Aaron stepped down off the train and was amazed when two red caps walked up to him and said,

"Sgt. Aaron Park, United States Army, allow us the honor to serve you."

Aaron's mouth was wide open because he was too surprised that anyone in Chicago knew his name let alone what train he was on. Aaron followed them through the lobby and out to a parking space designated "Visiting Dignitaries Only."

Only when the doors opened up, and Rose's Dad got out seconds before Rose, did he figure out what was going on. Rose's Dad thanked and started to tip the porters, but they refused, telling him it an honor to serve a Colored decorated US Army hero.

The trip back to Rose's home went by all too quickly. The ole man only worry was if either one was breathing since all they were doing was kissing. As they arrived, Aaron could see all of Rose's family on the front porch waving. This visit was going to be one hell of a family reunion.

After coffee and cake in the parlor and all proper introductions had been made, Rose's Mom said, "Rose Honey, Aaron must be tired. Why don't you show if up to the guest room." Rose's Mom knew her daughter, and Aaron needed some privacy if he was going to ask for her hand in marriage. Aaron had already written Rose's Dad to ask his permission. She knew her daughter well enough to know they would hear a high pitch scream when Aaron popped the question Rose had been waiting on for almost a year.

She was not wrong, bless the Lord.

The Wedding

Aaron was thrilled with to be reunited with his beloved Rose. The image of her on her parent's front porch the day he left her had kept him comforted during the long year building the Alaska Highway. Every GI misses someone. When you have found your soul mate, and an enemy has separated you from them, you had better lookout because nothing will stop them from getting home.

Every little girl has been planning their wedding day long before they even met their future husband. A very large binder crammed full of clipped articles, samples of the "perfect" cloth, the number and names of the bridesmaids (recorded in pencil) and of course, The Venue fill the pages. The planning goes into hyper drive when the girl is not the first in high school to be married. At future high school reunions, the "First to get Married" position is almost as coveted as homecoming queen and head cheerleader. Bragging rights are the mother's milk in gal pal circles, and the more items you have checked off the master Must Do list, the more conversations you will find yourself being the center of at that dreaded 10-year reunion.

Rose was no exception. She had a photo album full of newspaper articles from the wedding section of the Chicago paper; a dried up carnation from one of her close friends who had been married in High School before graduation. Her friend's marriage was hastily and unexpectedly announced, and the two were married in the middle of the week in her church. The girl and her new husband moved to the countryside so he could work on the farm for his uncle. She later gave birth to a 10 pound, 11-ounce boy four months premature. That baby boy was the damn biggest premie ever born in Cook County. Needless to say, Rose had BIG plans, and Mr. Porter had been saving for years so Rose could have everything she wanted.

All parents want to be grandparents, so no hill was too high to climb for their daughter.

The date had been set, and the invitations were printed. Aaron had even sent money to Monroe County Mississippi so his baby sister Carrie and his Mama could take the train from Memphis to Chicago.

Wren, Mississippi Winter 1942

Carrie's Mama got a letter from her soldier boy, Aaron. She always tore open the letter and stopped what she was doing to read about his adventures in Alaska. A western union money order with enough money for two tickets to Chicago was enclosed. The letter read,

"Mama, Rose and I are getting married, and I want you and Carrie to be here. Don't you worry about not having the perfect dress or shoes because Rose and her Mom will take you shopping when you arrive. I saved every dime I made up in Alaska and I want to pay for everything. I need to tell you how much I love and appreciate all you have done for me. I can't imagine a wedding without you and Carrie. Please say you will come. The Porters have plenty of room and want to meet you. Say you will come, please Mama.

Love Aaron."

Wild horses couldn't keep Aaron's mother away from his wedding. Besides, she had to give the future mother-in-law stamp of approval to Aaron before the wedding day. No Southern boy would ever consider marrying without this required step.

Baby sister Carrie was over the moon with excitement. She told all her friends in school that,

"I am going to Chicago to be in my big brother's wedding. He a war hero and built the Alaska Highway."

The teacher, Miss Davis, told Carrie to go to the big US map and point out Chicago so everybody could see where she was going for Christmas. The classmates crowded the blackboard where the big map hung on a rollup devise. Most didn't even know where they lived much less where a big city like Chicago was. Carrie, with a little help from Miss Davis, points to the big city on the Great Lakes. For most in the class, this was as close to economic freedom as they would ever see. But Carrie Park, sister of Sgt Aaron Park, US Army, was going to Chi-town for the holidays.

Back at Wedding Center, the Porter's Chicago Home

Rose and her Mom were in high gear planning the wedding of the year. Dresses had been selected, bridesmaids fitted (although a couple of the ladies needed quite more a bit of cloth than the rest), catering company contract signed and deposit paid, and the church booked. For those of you men that have never had the pleasure of watching your wife and daughter plan for "The Wedding", you have missed a valuable economic lesson that Milton Freedman couldn't demonstrate better. The military calls it mission creep, contractors call it cost overrun, and fathers call it,well, financial Armageddon. Once you have been on the check writing end of an out of control wedding planning disaster, you will NEVER be surprised by the government when they go over budget.

Wedding planning euphoria is cocaine for soon to be mother-in-laws. No expense is too much for their little girl who will soon bring home her first little grandbaby. All mothers dream of the grandkids first words being "Nana". The bills keep piling up because "this only happens once" and nothing is too good for "Princess".

Mr. Porter had taken going into to the den after supper to read and listen to the radio. His usual two fingers of bourbon had been supplanted by two larger glasses full of anything alcoholic. His only comment to Aaron was, "Take notes, my son because the apple doesn't fall far from the tree".

Aaron, of course, had no idea of what Mr. Porter meant because, let's face it, he was obsessed with visions of the upcoming wedding night.

Wren Mississippi

Word travels fast even in the days before widespread telephone service. In Alaska, it's called it The Bush Telegraph. In the South, it was just called Tuesday (or Friday, Monday,etc.). Everyone knew everyone's business and had plenty of time to give thoughtful insights and suggestions about folks comings and going ons, unsolicited of course. We all strive for the day when we have a perfect life so we, too, can help others with their sinful state of affairs.

Back at the Wren General Store AKA Gossip Central, Miss Lela Williams was busy passing judgment on all that needed it, so when the Uppity Park family came into the store, they became the next target. It would never cross her narrow little bigoted mind that

this was a big life event in their otherwise miserable lives for this
Colored family in the segregated South. The prideful Miss Lela
would have never seen any city north of Tupelo if it wasn't for the
merchandise buying trips to Memphis with the store owners son.
Most just figured she was better at bookkeeping than the boy's wife.
It always seemed road construction en route on Highway 78 always
caused the trip to last all day and late into the night.

"Mae, heard you and Carrie is heading to Chicago to see
Scooter get hitched. I guess he's done got too damn good to come
back to Wren. You better keep a close hand on that youngum of
yours, cause that fancy Yankee Colored crap don't fly down here in
Mississippi. You best not let him get above his raising. You hear me?"
the proud clerk said.

She looked around for approval from the pot belly stove and
checkers crew. They all nodded their heads up and down like those
little toy dogs with the springy heads people puts on the deck of the
rear car seats. Carl said to his pals, "Miss Lela sure put that Colored
woman in her place. Them Yankee states can do what the hell they
want to, but down here, we follow the preaching of the Good Book."

"Amen, Carl, Amen."

Aaron's Mama knew the score. Them white folks likes that,
"Yes, Sir Mr. Carl and you shore are right bout that" crap. Go along
to get along and pray for a better reward in heaven was her motto.

"I heard that, Miss Lela. You are so right. I afraid my boy
done had his head turned by some little Yankee princess. I never even
met her, but I'm sure she is bad for my boy. Scooter and me is gonna
have a us a "Come to Jesus" talking to when I gets up there."

Mae Park was a proud, strong woman and worth ten times of the likes of the racist store clerk. She thought,

Damn skinny white ass bitch wouldn't even have a job she wasn't the bastard child of the store owner. I remember her Mama, just white trash but a good person. She had to let the store owner have his way with her in the back room for store credit so she could feed her kids. He wasn't fooling anybody around here, except for that stupid cow of a wife of his who ain't playing with a full deck. She never leaves the house but twice a week. She does go to Sunday church and Wednesday night prayer meeting. She gets her hair done down at the beauty parlor on the way to prayer meeting. Beauty parlor my ass. Stupid white folks ought to find a new name for that place. Ain't been no beauty darken those doors in my recollection. I think "Pig Palace" would fit it better.

The Big Day Arrives

The Porter's church never looked as good as it did that fine December day in 1942. World War 2 was in full swing, 16 million American citizens were in uniform fighting and dying in foreign lands.

But in the tight-knit upscale Colored section of Chicago where the Porters called home, nothing matter more than Rose and Aaron's wedding. Aaron's Mama and baby sister, Carrie, had arrived several days earlier and were as ready as the rest of them. This trip was the first time any of Aaron's kinfolk had been outside the South. Things were as good as his Mama had heard. Nowhere up here could be found condescending white store clerks, or stupid fat redneck white men calling you names. The Porter's neighborhood was full of just nice warm houses where decent folks could make a living and raise a family.

As the organist played the wedding march, the whole congregation stood and turned to see Rose in her beautiful white dress come down the aisle on the arm of her father. Aaron had watched men die and before the war would be over, would see much worst. But the brave decorated war hero had a big smile on his face and a little tear in his eye. His best man was Rose's brother,who could not have been prouder of his sister's pick for a husband.

The reception hall was full of friends and family. The Porters were leaders in this community as well as in City Hall. The Mayor and the Chief of Police were in attendance, a testimony to Mr. Portes's standing in Chicago. Tables were full of the best food the neighborhood shops had to offer, some donated because of the service the Porter's had rendered to the area. Yes Sir, this spread could not be matched, not even on Chicago's North Shore. Soon, Rose emerged in a smart dress suit with Aaron in a three piece suit to say their goodbye before departing for their honeymoon. Carrie ran up to Aaron to hug him and thanks him for the trip of her life. Aaron told her to take care of Mama and stay strong.

As they drove off, Aaron's Mama wondered if see would ever see her son again. Her trip to the doctor back home had not gone well.

CHAPTER 16

OKINAWA, JAPAN IN APRIL 1945

The Army had deactivated everyone in the Colored Military Police Training Brigade at Camp Atterbury Indiana and reactivated them into combat Colored MP units reassigned to the Pacific Theater of Operation.

Aaron's unit was reassigned to Hawaii for duty with the 10th Army, a combination of Army and Marine Infantry Divisions. After limited combat during the Pacific island-hopping operation, which consisted of Marine units, their MP unit, a non-divisional asset of the 10th Army, was finally going to see its first major combat at the Japanese stronghold of Okinawa.

MP unit's duties during combat consisted of normal security in the company's AO (area of operation), some low-level intelligence gathering duties but most importantly was the marshaling and confinement of the POWs (prisoners of war). The treatment and rights of captured soldiers had been spelled out in the 1929 Geneva Convention Treaty, and this procedure was drilled into all the MPs trained at Camp Atterbury. The treaty stated that once any soldier surrendered they must be given food, clothing, and shelter for the duration of the war. Medical attention and regular visits by the International Red Cross was also guaranteed in addition to mail service from the captured serviceman's family. Aaron, Jim and the rest of the MP trainees were told both sides played by the same rulebook.

They would soon learn something different in the South Pacific.

The fighting on Okinawa was a long bloody battle that would last almost 90 days. During the worst part of the battle, VE Day (Victory in Europe) was announced on the Armed Services Radio, a lifeline to America for GIs. VE Day was a bittersweet day since the defeat of the Japs (VJ Day) seemed as far away as the moon. Of course, they were happy for all their buddies in Europe who was coming home. It hadn't been a picnic over there.

The Japs were dug into caves and ancient castle ruins and would fight to the death. They took no prisoners and could give a damn about the civilians on the Island. Control of the island according to the Brass (commanding officers and staff) was needed to launch an aerial attack on mainland Japan before the main invasion. If Okinawa was any indication of how determined the Japanese on the mainland were to repeal an attack, this phase of the war was just starting.

In some ironic twist of fate, the Okinawa operation started on 1 April 1945 which was both April Fool's Day and Easter Sunday. One had to assume that both a lot of faith and some foolish acts of bravery in combat would be needed to survive this battle.

Aaron was assigned to the 7th Infantry Division, which was sweeping across central Okinawa. All Divisions encountered fierce resistance from the enemy from fortified positions along one of the main highways, Route number 1. Aaron recalled at the time; he didn't know much of anything except he was getting shot at one hell of a lot. By the 8th of April, US troops had sustained casualties of 1500 while killing or capturing 4500 Japs. The intelligence officers (a contradiction of terms, like jumbo shrimp) worked their magic on the captured Japs. It was discovered that this battle had only captured the outposts and not the main stronghold of the enemy. Everyone settled in for a long drawn out bloody ordeal. An inexorable advance by the Allies would result in a high rate of casualties on both sides. The Japs sent civilians out in the line of fire to supply them with food and water that resulted in many senseless civilian deaths. Toward the end of the battle, as many as 150,000 Okinawa civilians committed suicide by jumping to their deaths from high cliffs or by other methods. The Japs had told them untrue horror stories of what the invaders would do to them if they were captured alive. The lying sons of bitches were simply telling them exactly what they had done to the Chinese men and women in Nanking only a few years before. The Japs raped men, women, girls (pregnant or not), forced family members to commit incest with their wives, sisters, and daughters for the amusement of the Japs troops. According to some reports, once some of the pregnant women were raped, their fetuses were cut out of the womb and killed. The horror stories caused the mass suicide of almost a third of the civilian population on Okinawa. The sad fact was the stories were just the unspeakable horrors the Japs had committed to the Chinese people during 1937 and 1938 in Nanking, China.

All Japanese captives were afforded all the rights of the Geneva Convention Treaty, while the US military was fully aware of the inhuman treatment of our troops and allies in the Philippines. Aaron was stationed at a POW compound. Aaron had decided not ever to talk about his war experiences with his family. It was best his wife and children didn't know what man was capable of doing to other human beings. Some US soldiers on Okinawa surrendered to the Japs thinking they would be treated as POWs. Aaron had discovered the bodies of a squad of missing GIs who had been captured, tortured, disemboweled and shot by these Japs. No Geneva Convention Treaty treatment was given to these brave soldiers by their Japanese captors. Aaron's unit treated the captured Jap fighters on Okinawa with some humanity. Well, he did most of the time.

CHAPTER 17

THE END IS IN SIGHT

The battle for Okinawa was over but mainland Japan was another thing. As successful and necessary as D-Day was to defeat Hitler, it had been costly regarding men and equipment. But the invasion of Japan would make D-Day look like a training maneuver. The local Japanese population had been told about what the Americans would do to them, so they were prepared to fight to the last man, woman, and child.

On Tinian Island in the Mariana Islands Chain was a US Army Air Corp Base where bombing runs over mainland Japan had been conducted since recapturing Guam and Saipan. Boeing B-17 Flying Fortresses and B-29 Super Fortresses had dropped enough ordinance to blow a hole big enough to fit Lake Michigan into without a hint of surrender from the Emperor. Some alternative to an invasion was required. Europe had been an Allied victory thanks to FDR and Churchill's Europe First policy and the US just wanted to bring the boys back home. No civilian, politician, or serviceman wanted a prolonged land battle on the Japanesse mainland.

On May 8, 1945, Aaron and his buddies had listened to Armed Forces Radio announce the war was over in Europe, VE Day. Everyone was happy for their friends and relatives who had been fighting in Europe knowing they would going home, a wish every single serviceman wanted more than anything.

But the unconditional surrender of Japan was paramount to ending the Second World War. Boeing Aircraft Company had designed and built many of the warbirds that had gotten us as close to total victory as we were in August 1945. Boeing had one more ace up their sleeve, the B-29 Super Fortress. These new bombers were game changers. The B-29 crews could fly in their uniforms and not all bundled up in leather and wool. These new bombers were pressurized and could reach altitudes of over 35,000, well above the service ceiling of any Jap interpreter airplanes. Japan was a sitting duck and Army Air Corp Commander Curtis "Bombs Away" LeMay was pounding them back to feudal days. He had firebombed Tokyo and set their wooden structures on fire. The Operation Meetinghouse firebombing of Tokyo on the night of **9** March 1945 had been the single deadliest air raid of World War II. Over 100,000 civilians had died, but the military ruler, Hideki Tojo, refused to surrender. With nothing left to bomb with conventional weapons, the US needed a bigger, better bomb.

On May 19, 1945, a new, secretive organization began arriving at North Field, Tinian; the 1,767-man 509th Composite Group headed by Col. Paul W. Tibbets, Jr. The other airmen on Tinian ridiculed the men of the new air group because they hadn't been assigned any risky missions. Soon they would have to eat some crow.

Army MP HQ Okinawa

The milk run from Hawaii had been delayed several times
in the past month due to other more important missions. Mail call
for a deployed soldier was more important than chow and sleep.
The only thing that even came close to letters from home was a
hot shower and a clean uniform. Aaron went to mail call that day
expecting letters from Rose, and he wasn't disappointed. The mail
clerk yelled out,

Sgt. Aaron Park. Come and get your mail!

Aaron was hoping to receive some long overdue mail from
Rose since routine "milk" runs had been halted for some unknown
reason. The sixth day of August 1945 would be remembered by
every serviceman serving in the Pacific. The Enola Gay B-29
dropped the first nuclear bomb on freedom's enemy, Japan.
The ***Enola Gay*** left runway 1 at North Field and dropped an
atomic bomb on the city of Hiroshima, Japan, which in a matter of
seconds destroyed 62,000 buildings and killed or mortally wounded
80,000 people.

On August 9, Maj. Charles W. Sweeney, flying from Tinian
in the B-29 ***Bock's Car***, dropped a second atomic bomb on Nagasaki,
bad weather having prevented his attacking the primary target,
Kokura. Soon after, the Japanese surrendered.

The Second World War was over, and soon most would be
going home and discharged from the service. Only after VJ Day,
could the millions of men in uniform seriously start thinking about
life after the War.

Aaron thought,

> *Damn right, you Jap bastards. Two mushroom*
> *clouds over Japan looks damn good to us soldiers*
> *on Okinawa. No need to waste any more American*
> *men's life fighting the Japs. I'm going home to*
> *Chicago to be with Rose. All I got to say is, "Don't*
> *start a war if you can't take the heat."*

Soon, the war will be over. The Japnesse Emperior Hiroheto would sign the unconditional surrender on the deck of the battleship, USS Missouri as General Douglas MacArthor watched. The bebuilding of Europe and Japan could begin.

Aaron had some catching up to do since Rose had sent him at least twenty new letters. Aaron always made sure he read them in the order Rose had written them so not to miss anything. It had taken him three days to read the last letter. Rose started out by saying, Daddy had lined him up a job interview with the Chicago Chief of Police. Rose went on to say, she and her Mom had been painting and remodeling the bedroom next to their room.

Still as clueless as most men are, Aaron continued to read on wondering, **"Where the hell is that woman of mine going in this letter?"**

The last sentence said,

"Aaron Park, you keep your Colored butt safe and come home safe and sound. I ain't raising your child alone. Love Rose."

The End

Or is it?

Read the next chapter of Aaron Park's saga in
Monroe County Murder, on sale now at Amazon
and in all fine well-managed bookstores.

ABOUT THE AUTHOR

Mike Dryden was born in Monroe County, Mississippi in the late forties. He graduated from Amory High School in the sixties and Mississippi State University with a BS in Education. He was commissioned a second lieutenant in the US Army and attended Rotary Wing Qualification School. He was assigned to the 101st Airborne Division at Fort Campbell, Kentucky as a helicopter pilot and aviation logistic maintenance officer. He left active duty and continued his military career until 1998 when he retired as a Major. He worked in a variety of jobs ranging from test pilot to ad salesperson until his retirement. He received a Master of Aeronautical Science from Embry-Riddle Aeronautical University and is a dual rated instrument commercial pilot. He has worked in both secondary and adult education fields in Alaska for the past fourteen years. He served as public affairs officer for the Alaska Wing Civil Air Patrol, editor of the Alaska CAP Wing Tips magazine and a mission pilot on search and rescue missions. He presently serves on the board of the Older Person Action Group and writes a monthly article on veterans' health care issues in the Senior Voice newspaper. He also has contributed to the Stars and Stripes Alaska military newspaper on a broad range of subjects. His latest articles include a series of the contributions of the black soldiers during World War ll and the construction of the Alaska Highway. He is a volunteer for the State of Alaska Long-Term Care Ombudsman program where he advocates senior citizens rights residing in elder care facilities. He spends his spare time flying, substitute teaching traveling and writing fiction and non-fiction works.

Made in the USA
Monee, IL
10 October 2022